Anonymous

The Southern Planter

Vol. 19

Anatiposi

Anonymous

The Southern Planter

Vol. 19

Reprint of the original, first published in 1859.

1st Edition 2023 | ISBN: 978-3-38231-168-1

Anatiposi Verlag is an imprint of Outlook Verlagsgesellschaft mbH.

Verlag (Publisher): Outlook Verlag GmbH, Zeilweg 44, 60439 Frankfurt, Deutschland
Vertretungsberechtigt (Authorized to represent): E. Roepke, Zeilweg 44, 60439 Frankfurt, Deutschland
Druck (Print): Books on Demand GmbH, In de Tarpen 42, 22848 Norderstedt, Deutschland

THE

SOUTHERN PLANTER,

A MONTHLY PERIODICAL

DEVOTED TO

Agriculture, Horticulture,

AND THE

HOUSEHOLD ARTS.

AUGUST & WILLIAMS, Proprietors.
J. E. WILLIAMS, Editor.

VOL. NINETEEN.

PRINTED AT RICHMOND, VIRGINIA,
BY MACFARLANE & FERGUSSON.
1859.

VOL. XIX. [JANUARY.] **No. 1.**

PUBLISHED MONTHLY. AUGUST & WILLIAMS, PROPRIETORS.

J. E. WILLIAMS, EDITOR.

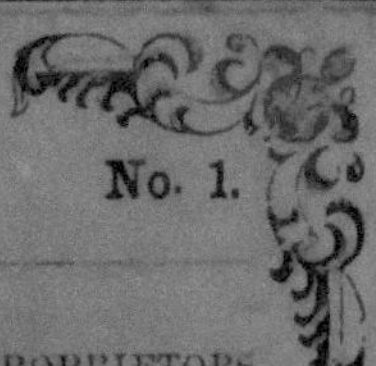

THE SOUTHERN PLANTER.

DEVOTED TO

AGRICULTURE, HORTICULTURE,

AND THE

HOUSEHOLD ARTS.

PRINTED AT RICHMOND, VA.,
BY MACFARLANE & FERGUSSON.
1859.

CONTENTS.

THE SOUTHERN PLANTER

Is published monthly, in sixty-four octavo pages, upon the following *Terms*:

TWO DOLLARS AND FIFTY CENTS per annum, unless paid in *advance*.

Advance payments as follows:

One copy, one year, - $2
Six copies, do - 10
Thirteen copies, one year, - 20
Twenty do do - 30
One copy, three years, - 5

And one copy free to persons sending us the NAMES and MONEY for thirteen or more new subscribers.

All money remitted to us will be considered at our risk *only*, when the letter containing the same shall have been *registered*. This rule is adopted not for our protection, but for the protection of our correspondents, and we wish it distinctly understood that we take the risk only when this condition is complied with.

ADVERTISEMENTS

Will be inserted at the following rates:

Business Cards of 5 lines or less, per annum, $5 00

One-eighth of a column.	1st insertion,	1 00
	Each continuance,	75
	6 months, without	4 00
	12 " alteration,	7 50
One fourth of a column,	1st insertion.	1 75
	Each continuance,	1 25
	6 months, without	7 50
	12 " alteration,	14 00
One-half of a column,	1st insertion.	3 25
	Each continuance,	2 50
	6 months, without	14 00
	12 " alterations,	25 00
One column, or Half a page	1st insertion,	6 00
	Each continuance,	4 50
	6 months, without	25 00
	12 " alteration,	40 00
One page,	1st insertion,	10 00
	Each continuance,	7 50
	6 months, without	40 00
	12 " alteration,	70 00

Advertisements out of the city must be accompanied with the money or city references to insure insertion

---

R. M. NIMMO,
GENERAL AGENT & STOREKEEPER
OF THE
VIRGINIA PENITENTIARY,
No. 27 PEARL STREET.

Keeps constantly on hand a supply of the following articles manufactured at the Penitentiary of the most faithful and substantial manner: BOOTS, SHOES, BROGUES, HARNESS, KERSEYS, LINSEYS, COTTONS, BAGS, WAGONS, CARTS, WHEELBARROWS, AXES, &c.

Orders Promptly Executed.

Nov 1858—tf

FRUIT TREES & SHRUBBERY.
SOUTHERN GREENWOOD NURSERY.

Having on hand a choice variety of FRUIT TREES of my own raising and grafting, sufficiently large for transplanting, I respectfully call the attention of the public to them.

My NURSERY is located one and a half miles northeast from the Old Market, where I will take pleasure in showing them.

All orders addressed to, or left at my agents, Messrs. Van Lew, Taylor & Co., No. 19 Main St., Richmond, Va., or myself, will meet with prompt attention.

Sept 1858—tf   LEWIS TUDOR.

BUIST'S ALMANAC AND GARDEN MANUAL FOR 1859,

Is now ready. It is designed to furnish concise hints to the Farmer and Cottager on VEGETABLE, FRUIT and FLOWER culture, with select lists of the most approved varieties, &c., &c., gratis, on application, or mailed on the receipt of a letter stamp.

R. BUIST, Nurseryman and Seed Grower. Seed and Horticultural Warehouse, Nos. 922 and 924 Market St., Philadelphia.   dec 58—4t

---

Corn Shellers of Various Kinds.

The Cylinder for hand will shell 400 bushels per day, the same for horse power and hand will shell the same by hand and 600 by horse power. The Reading Sheller will shell from 1,000 to 1,500 bushels.

WHEAT FANS, and the usual variety of machinery on hand.   H. M. SMITH,
oc 58—tf   14 Main Street.

PURE NORTH DEVONS.

A Bull and Heifer, each 17 months old, and a Bull Calf 4 months old. Also a Cow 5 years old, with a Heifer Calf 2 months old, deliverable at Tolersville, on the Virginia Central Railroad, or if preferred, at any other point on said Road.

To any gentleman who wants a cross, or otherwise to breed these beautiful cattle, so well adapted to the light soils of Eastern Virginia, I would recommend the 17 months bull. Price of same, $75.

Address, Tolersville, Louisa County, Va.
dec 58—3t   P. B. PENDLETON.

Devoted to Agriculture, Horticulture, and the Household Arts.

Agriculture is the nursing mother of the Arts.
[Xenophon.

Tillage and Pasturage are the two breasts of the State.—Sully.

J. E. WILLIAMS, Editor.

AUGUST & WILLIAMS, Prop'rs.

Vol. XIX.   RICHMOND, VA., JANUARY, 1859.   No. 1.

English Agriculture.

We return our thanks to Sam'l Sands, Esq., of Baltimore, for the following interesting account of various agricultural experiments, published in the Baltimore American.

We take this occasion to call the attention of all farmers to the agency established in Baltimore, by Mr. Sands, for the purchase and sale of lands—live stock, &c. For full information in regard to the objects of this agency, see the card of Mr. S. in our advertising columns.

—

LETTER FROM DR. GERARD RALSTON.

London, September 15, 1858.

Messrs. Dobbin & Fulton :—A few days ago I made an excursion, with some American gentlemen, to the most interesting country-seat of the liberal and public spirited English country gentleman, John Bennett Lawes, Esq., near Harpenden, twenty miles from London, and a few miles beyond the ancient and most interesting city of St. Albans, (celebrated for its magnificent Abbey, nearly the largest and most beautiful of the churches of England) and entering the park of Rothamstead, we soon discovered that we were visiting an old-fashioned but most beautiful and well maintained country-seat of a wealthy landed proprietor. Driving through the park, which abounds with large Elms, Oak, Ash, Lime, Beech, Birch, Acacia, Plane and other beautiful trees, and seeing numerous sheep and cattle which, in my opinion, ornamented the park far more than useless deer, which I am sorry to say, too often encumber the parks of the gentry of England, we arrived at the venerable Hall, an ancient mansion of about three hundred and fifty years old, which, on examining we 'found to contain every thing that wealth and luxury could make conducive to the comfort of its residents. We found the walls of its drawing-room, &c., decorated with the landscapes and other pictures of its tasteful mistress, and its hall was ornamented with the spoils of the chase of its excellent master ; but, leaving the house and walking over the soft Turkey carpet-like lawn, admiring the flower-beds, shrubbery and beautiful grounds, we entered an avenue of old Lime trees, under whose delightfully odorous boughs, we took a refreshing lunch, and then proceeding under the guidance of our scientific and courteous hosts, Dr. Gilbert, (Doctor of Philosophy and Fellow of the Chemical Society) and Dr. Evan Pugh, of Westchester, Pennsylvania, we examined the experimental farm which is so celebrated, not only in these Islands, but throughout the Continent also, for developing agricultural improvement. At this place Mr. Lawes owns about 1,800 acres of land, in addition to some estates in Scotland, of which 1,630 acres are employed as arable land, and for farming purposes, and 100 acres are purely what is called the park, and devoted to grass and the pleasure grounds only. The remainder, or 70 acres, are used for scientific agricultural experiments for ascertaining what are the laws of vegetable growth and nutrition, in order to fully understand how to raise a maximum crop at a minimum expense.

What we first examined was under a glass roof and protected from the wind at the sides by a screen, a number of plants, including the most commonly cultivated cereal and leguminous and root crops, growing in tin vessels, with 40 lbs. of soil each, and the plant issuing at top through a small hole in a glass plate, which is soldered on to the top so as to prevent any evaporation from the soil, except that which goes off through the leaves of the plant. The pot is weighed when the seed is planted, as so also is all the water added during its growth, at the termination of which the crop is dried and weighed, and the amount of dried matter in it compared with the amount of water evaporated from the leaves. It is found that for every part of dry matter freed, 250 parts of water pass through the leaves, or for every ton of wheat or grass produced upon a field, 250 tons of water must have been evaporated from the vegetable matter producing it. Or for a field of grass producing 3 tons per acre, 750 tons (about 500 barrels) of water must have passed off from every acre. This points to the cause of the good effect of rain, and the damage of drought—shewing the dependance of the former upon the seasons.

We next examined the effect of different manures upon grass; 17 lots, of one-half an acre each, have been under experimentation for the last 4 years. The result shows the natural produce of the ground (which has not been ploughed or showed for the last two hundred years, and which has only natural grasses upon it) is for this years, per acre, 1 ton, 2 hundred weight, 20 pounds. This is not increased by 2,000 lbs. of sawdust just beside it on another plat. But 14 tons of barn-yard manure per acre produced 2 tons

7 cwt., 2 qrs. Rye grass, soft broom grass, Bent grass were particularly developed, while worthless grasses, as Quaking grass, Dogstail grass and several weeds, (Plaintain, &c.) were either entirely lost or much diminished in quantity. An addition of 2,000 lbs. of sawdust produced no effect on the manure plat. An addition of 400 lbs. of salts of ammonia (the sulphate and muriate of ammonia) per acre gives 1 ton, 15 cwt., 2 qrs. and 6 pounds. And mineral salts (sulphates of potash 300 lbs., of soda 200 lbs., of magnesia 100 lbs., and 200 lbs. of boneash, with 150 lbs. of sulphuric acid) give 1 ton, 16 cwt. 1 qr. 22 lbs. Sawdust has no effect on either of the latter, but the latter, on addition of 400 pounds of ammonia salts gives 3 tons, 4 hundred weight 0 qrs. 4 pounds. The addition of 800 lbs. of ammonia salts gives 3 tons, 7 cwt. 0 qrs. 4 lbs. Other results are equally striking, but the most remarkable fact is the change produced in the quality of the grass by these manurial substances. The sawdust has no effect whatever, either upon the quantity or the quality of the grass. All the substances which give much increase, tend to keep down the weeds. The mineral salts, the sulphates, with phosphates, tend largely to develop the leguminous plants; clover, lotus, lucerne, &c., were here developed in a marked degree. The large increase of ammonia, whether with or without minerals, showed the development of large quantities of heavier and coarser grasses, as Dactylus glomerata, and Bromus mollis. These experiments, when carried out with great care and exactness for a series of years, will supply a rich store of information as to the value of different manurial substances for the promotion of different kinds of grasses. Not only are the statistics with regard to crops and manures kept, but small plats, are selected in each plat, and in these each kind of grass is planted and the amount weighed, so that the exact relation between the several quantities produced may be recorded.

EXPERIMENTAL WHEAT FIELD.

There are 40 plats, each containing three-tenths of an acre, on which wheat has been grown continuously under different circumstances for the last 15 years. It would be impossible here to enter into the details of these experiments. Several elaborate papers have already appeared in the journal of the Royal Agricultural Society of England, in which the statistics here obtained are given, and from which, conclusions have been drawn that have elicited much discussion, both in England and Germany. It is found that on this soil, which is a rather heavy clay interspersed with the chalk flints, the continuous yield without manure is about 18 bushels per acre. The addition of ammonia salts without minerals for 15 years has at last so far exhausted the mineral constituents in the soil, that the produce by such salts now is not as great as formerly, yet it now gives 30 bushels per acre. The addition of mineral salts, (sulphate of potash 300 pounds, of soda 200 lbs., of magnesia 100 lbs. and bone ash 200 lbs., with sulphuric acid 150 lbs.) scarcely raises the unmanured plat above its normal amount (20 to 24 bushels per acre being thus obtained.) But other plats showing the effect of the different quantities of ammonia with these minerals are most marked. The addition of 200 lbs. of ammoniacal salts per acre with these mineral salts, gives for 1857 (this year 1858 results being not yet ready) thirty-five bushels per acre; four hundred pounds of ammoniacal salts with minerals 46 bushels per acre; 600 lbs. of ammoniacal salts with minerals 50 bushels per acre, but this large quantity is liable to fall down, owing to the great development of straw. The great point claimed for these experiments is, that they show that the atmospheric sources of nitrogen (or ammonia) are not "amply sufficient for the purpose of agriculture" as has been contended by some. They also point out the great value of the highly nitrogenised manures, or the Peruvian guanos, &c.

EXPERIMENTAL BARLEY FIELD.

There are also twenty-four plats of one-sixth of an acre each. These have been going on for seven years upon the same land. They also show results corresponding to those just noticed. Unmanured plats about half a crop, (29 bushels;) with 14 tons of barnyard manure a good crop, 51 bushels per acre; mineral manures; (sulphate of soda, potash and magnesia,) about half a crop (32 bushels;) super-phosphate of lime, a little more, (33 bushels;) (super-phosphate of lime and sulphurate of soda, potash and magnesia,) yet more, (39 bushels;) nitrate of soda (Chili saltpetre,) gives 47 bushels; ammonia salts, about a like quantity, and a mixture of all the minerals (alkalies and phosphates,) and ammonia salt, gives 57 bushels per acre.

Which latter number, points to what purely artificial manures are capable of doing. The crop is about double : "two straws are made to grow where but one grew before." It also points to the fact that the crop is not produced by any *one substance*, that no *quack nostrum* or stimulant can be put upon land by which it will be made to produce without all these various constituents applied to get this 57 bushels of barley per acre. If any one of these substances produces an effect it is because the other substances already exists in the soil, ready to act in concert with it. The experiments show that nitrogen and phosphoric acid are most generally deficient in soils; and hence the addition of these substances produced great results; not that *they* alone do it, but because they were the only substances failing in the soil, and without them nothing can be produced. They are but two links in the middle of a chain, without which the chain has no strength, but *they are not the whole chain* as a superficial observer might be led to suppose.

5th. Other experiments were made with beans and turnips, but they are ommitted for the present.

7th. We next go to the Laboratory. Here is a fine building erected by the farmers of England, at an expense of upwards of 7,000 dollars, and presented to Mr. Lawes as a testimonial of his liberality and of his great services in Agricultural Chemistry. It is most admirably fitted up with sands-baths, water-baths, muffle furnaces, &c., &c., drying-rooms, &c., &c., for all the various operations of drying, analysing, &c., &c., of the products of the experimental fields. The different grains and root crops are dried, the amount of ash determined, and put away for analysis. The elaborate system of shelves and cupboards are full of specimens of ash of grain and straw ready for further investigation. An extensive collection of preparations of the different parts of animals including the fat, the flesh, the bones, the tendrons, &c., &c., of all the different organs of the animal body. These had been used in an extensive investigation involving the slaughter and careful cutting up and weighing of some hundred head of cattle, hogs and sheep, by which, when taken into connection with the statistics of food eaten by them, the relative value of the different kinds of food to produce fat, flesh, &c., &c., would be ascertained.

8th. Dr. Evan Pugh's own experiments.

Explanation.—"No non-nitrogenized substance can form an element of nutrition."—*Baron Liebig.*

Animals can't live without nitrogenous foods. Animals must live on vegetables; hence vegetables must be nitrogenous.—They must get their nitrogen from the air, or soil, or from both. They must get the form of *pure nitrogen gas*, of which air contains 78 per cent., or they must get it from compounds of nitrogen, of which the most common are nitric acid and ammonia. From which of all these sources (air or earth, the pure nitrogen gas, the ammonia, or the nitric acid) do plants get their nitrogen? The importance of this question is heightened by the high price of nitrogenous manures. If plants can get nitrogen from the exhaustable resources of the free nitrogen gas of the air, why not seek to find the circumstances under which it is obtained, and avoid paying for saltpetre, guano and other nitrogenous manures? It must be decided whether plants are capable of assimilating the free nitrogen at all. To do this our countryman, Dr. Pugh, came to Rothamstead.

The plants experimented upon must be grown in a soil and an atmosphere, free from nitrogenous compounds, must be evolved with water containing no such compound, and then the plant so grown analysed, to see if it contained any more nitrogen than the seed contained. To free the soil from nitrogen it was heated red hot for several hours in an iron muffle, and then washed with pure water for several days, and finally ignited simultaneously with peat, and the ash of the plant to be grown in it. The red hot soil and red hot ash were then brought into the red hot pot, and well mixed and allowed to cool under a large glass vessel set in sulphuric acid so that no ammonia of the air could get to the soil. Once cooled down, pure water was added, and the seeds of known weight and per centage of nitrogen were planted, and the whole removed to large glass shades, 3 feet high and 10 inches diameter. These shades rested in grooves filled with mercury at the bottom, so that all communication with the external air was cut off. By aid of bent glass tubes going down into the groove through the quick silver under the glass shade and rising in the inside of the vessel, water and air free from ammonia were supplied to the plant. By a complicated system of bottles partly filled with sulphuric acid and tubes with pumice wet with this acid, the air supplied was purified from ammonia, and by passing a stream of water from a cistern into a close vessel, from which the air only could pass out though a tube leading into these bottles, a constant steam of ammonia, free air is passed to the plant. In this way 18 different vessels are arranged, in which wheat, barley, oats, beans, peas, clover, tobacco are grown, some with no ammonia, others with measured quantities, to see if a gain takes place by assimilation of nitrogen from the air. The plants to which no nitrogen was given, and which contained no more than that contained in the seed, were only a few inches high; those to which combined nitrogen (sulphurate of ammonia) had been given, were five to ten times as high; thus showing that the plant could not grow without the aid of combined nitrogen—in other words that the nitrogen of air cannot be assimilated. But before this point can be settled with accuracy, the whole crop, the whole soil and the pot must be analysed to see if the entire nitrogen thus found agrees with that in the seed, *plus* what was added. This will take much work yet.

Other points are the gas found in plants. By a simple piece of apparatus the work of getting the gas out of a plant is reduced to that of a few minutes. Quicksilver is made to run out of a vacuum and this is brought in communication with a vessel filled with water, (that has been boiled to free it from air) in which the plant is placed. The air rushes out into the vacuum with great rapidity, and in ten minutes can be collected.—This I saw done. The gas was then analysed and shown to consist of carbonic acid, nitrogen and oxygen in very different proportions from what is given in the books upon this subject. This method will be very useful for all cases of getting gasses from plants, from fluids, or from animal secretions and excretions. Dr. Pugh has already made some hundred analyses of the gas plants, and hopes to follow up the investigations when he returns to America. On our way to the Laboratory we saw an extensive field, which the the liberal proprietor of Rothamstead, has set aside for allotments of three-fourths of an acre to one and a quarter acres each for each family of his work people who cultivate their vegetables during the intervals of labor, and in this way are prevented from going to the beer-houses—the bane of working classes of England. Mr. Lawes has, most munificiently, also built a very tasteful and convenient club-house, which is well warmed and lighted and abounds in books, papers, &c., and where a very sensible and pious clergyman preaches on Sunday evenings, so as not to interfere with the Church of England services during the day. This establishment also offers a powerful rivalry to the beer-house and gives additional motives for the greatful feelings of the people of Harpenden towards their benevolent and public spirited Lord of the Manor, Mr. Lawes.

The plain farmer of America may inquire of what good are all these elaborate experiments? What is the use of this science, and this extended investigation into the products of the earth? A great many discoveries of an important practical kind have been made; a series of experiments, both on the growth of the most important crops, and the feeding of animals for the production of meat and manure, has been gone through. As to the first of these questions, the course adopted was to grow by different chemical manures some of the most important crops year after year on the same land—for example, the cereals, the leguminous crops and the root crops, and at the same time, to grow experimentally the same crops one after the other, in the order in which they would follow each other in rotation. In like manner vast series of experiments had been made on the connection between the amount of food consumed by fattening of animals, and the increase and manure which they yielded for that food, and many of the results have been published in the journals of the Royal Agricultural Society, and in pamphlets and publications which have been followed by great benefit to the community. The practical result is, that this and other old farms in this country, that have been under constant cultivation for upwards of 1,000 years, produce from 48 to 58 bushels of wheat per acre, whilst the farms of New York and Pennsylvania, which have been under culture for only 50 or 60 or 75 or 100 years, are constantly diminishing in produce, and our fellow-townsman, Henry Carey, in his most interesting letters to President Buchanan, published this year, (1858) says that 12 and 15 bushels of wheat are now produced, where formerly 25, 28, and 30 bushels were grown. So of barley, of Indian corn, of tobacco, of cotton and other articles, whether they be products of the North or South, or the East or West. This retro-grade movement in our agriculture *must be checked*, and I am happy to say that our fellow-statesman, the scientific, energetic, persevering and most zealous and successful analytic and chemical agriculturist, Dr. Pugh, of Chester County, Pennsylvania, is the very person to teach our farmers how to recover the ground they have lost, and to make our fields in Montgomery, Berks, Lancaster, Chester, Delaware, &c., &c., in Pennsylvania and all over the United States, produce as good crops as are common in Norfolk, Berks, Hertfordshire, &c., in England, which have been in constant cultivation since the time of the Romans.

I am glad to say Dr. Pugh is soon to return home. He has been attending the Universities and Agricultural Colleges of the Continent for some time, and also has made most diligent inquiry into the best farming practices of the Continent. He has been at Harpenden for two years, and in connection with the learned, scientific and experienced Dr. Gilbert, who is the chief of the Laboratory, and of the scientific staff for carrying out the magnificent experiments of the liberal and enlightened Mr. Lawes, who has been spending for the last fifteen years an average of £1,500 per annum purely in scientific and economical investigations. Dr. Pugh has profited much by the opportunities he has had at Harpenden, and I hope when he returns home he will be induced to establish an Agricultural College, to teach all the sciences and all the practice that are required by our rural population to enable them, not only to prevent a further decline in agriculture, but by the application of suitable manures and the proper treatment of the land, to restore the fertility of the soil, so that we may again have, not only 25 to 30 bushels of wheat per acre, but have this product advanced to 50 or 55 bushels, which is by no means uncommon in many of the counties of this old and long cultivated country, and if it had been treated as badly as Virginia has been, would now be a worn out and exhausted and miserable country, with its 4 or 5 bushels of wheat only to the acre.

Dr. Pugh has been remarkably fortunate in making the acquaintance of such gentlemen as Mr. Lawes and Dr. Gilbert, who in the development of agricultural improvement, have been of inestimable value to this country, and I may add, to Europe. Mr. Lawes being a man of great public spirit and of most enlightened mind, and being blessed with a very large fortune, (say $50,000 per annum,) has, with a zeal and patriotism beyond praise, devoted at least $7,500 per annum, for the last fifteen years, to the improvement of agriculture, and Dr. Gilbert, with all the science that could be procured from the best education, from Baron Liebig, and other eminent chemical agriculturists, and from other sources, which his investigating spirit has found out, and is every way qualified to assist our enterprising countryman in his investigations, and he has accordingly taken advantage of the ample resources furnished by the liberal minded Mr. Lawes and the devoted (to scientific investigation) Dr. Gilbert, to make experiments, which he has not yet given to the world, but which, I hope, when made known to our countrymen, will incite to an improvement of agriculture, which will be of inestimable benefit to our country. Dr. Pugh returns soon to Pennsylvania. I hope his success will be as complete as his great merit entitles him to.

I am, very respectfully, yours,
GERARD RALSTON.

From the Valley Farmer.

The Way to Wealth.

Benjamin Franklin, the self-taught American philosopher, was perhaps the most extraordinary man that this country has ever produced. It may be impossible to gather from the history and labours of one individual mind more practical wisdom and varied instruction than he has given to the world. For many years he published the Pennsylvania Almanac, called Poor Richard (Saunders) and furnished it with many wise sayings and proverbs which related to topics of "industry, attention to one's own business, and frugality." The most of these he finally collected and digested in the following general preface, which sayings are so peculiarly adapted to the present times, that we do not know that we can do our readers better service than to give them a place in the *Valley Farmer.* These sayings were not more applicable to the people and the times one hundred years ago than to the present, and their teachings should never be lost sight of, until the world is much wiser and better than it is at present:

The Way to Wealth, as clearly Shown in the Preface of an old Pennsylvania Almanac, entitled "Poor Richard Improved."

"COURTEOUS READER:—I have heard that nothing gives an author so great pleasure as to find his works quoted respectfully by others, then, how much I must have been gratified by an incident I am going to relate to you. I stopped my horse lately where a great number of people were collected at an auction of merchant's goods. The hour of the sale not being come, they were conversing on the badness of the times; and one of the company called to a plain, clean old man with white locks, "Pray, Father Abraham, what think you of the times? Will not these heavy taxes quite ruin the country? How shall we be able to pay them? What would you advise us to?" Father Abraham stood up and replied: "If you would have my advice, I will give it you in short, for 'a word to the wise is enough,' as Poor Richard says." They joined in desiring him to speak his mind, and, gathering around him, he proceeded as follows:

"Friends," said he, "the taxes are indeed very heavy, and if those laid on by the government were the only ones we had to pay, we might more easily discharge them, but we have many others, and much more grievous ones to some of us. We are taxed twice as much by our idleness, three times as much by our pride, and four times as much by our folly; and from these taxes the commissioners cannot ease or deliver us, by allowing an abatement. However, let us hearken to good advice, and something may be done for us; 'God helps them that help themselves,' as Poor Richard says.

"I. It would be thought a hard government that should tax its people one-tenth part of their time to be employed in its service, but idleness taxes many of us much more; sloth, by bringing on disease, absolutely shortens life. 'Sloth, like rust, consumes faster than labour wears, while the used key is always bright,' as Poor Richard says. 'But dost thou love life, then do not squander time, for that is the stuff life is made of,' as Poor Richard says. How much more than is necessary do we spend in sleep, forgetting that 'The sleeping fox catches no poultry,' and 'That there will be sleeping enough in the grave,' as Poor Richard says.

"If time be of all things the most precious, wasting time must be,' as Poor Richard says, 'the greatest prodigality,' since, as he elsewhere tells us, 'Lost time is never found again; and what we call time enough, always proves little enough.' Let us, then, up and be doing, and doing to the purpose; so by diligence we shall do more with less perplexity. Sloth makes all things difficult, but industry all easy, and he that riseth late must trot all day, and shall scarce overtake his business at night, while Laziness travels so slowly, that Poverty soon overtakes him. 'Drive thy business, let not that drive thee, and early to bed and early to rise, makes a man healthy, wealthy and wise,' as Poor Richard says.

"So what signifies wishing and hoping for better times? We make these times better if we bestir ourselves. 'Industry need not wish, and he that lives upon hopes will die fasting. There are no gains without pains; then help, hands, for I have no lands, or, if I have, they are smartly taxed. He that hath a trade hath an estate, and he that hath a calling hath an office of profit and honour,' as Poor Richard says; but then the trade must be worked at, and the calling followed, or neither the estate nor the office will enable us to pay our taxes. If we are industrious we shall never starve; for, 'At the working-man's house hunger looks in but dares not enter.' Nor will the bailiff or the constable enter; for 'Industry pays debts, while despair increaseth them.' What though you have found no treasure, nor has any rich relation left you a legacy? 'Diligence is the mother of luck, and God gives all things to industry. 'Then plow deep while sluggards sleep, and you shall have corn to sell and to keep.' Work while it is called to-day, for you know not how much you may be hindered to-morrow. 'One day to-day is worth two to-morrows,' as Poor Richard says, and further, 'Never leave that till to-morrow which you can do to-day.' If you were a servant, would you not be ashamed that a good master should catch you idle? Are you, then, your own master? Be ashamed to catch yourself idle when there is so much to be done for yourself, your family and your country. Handle your tools without mittens; remember that 'The cat in gloves catches no mice,' as Poor Richard says. It is true there is much to be done, and perhaps you are weak-handed, but stick to it steadily, and you will see great effects, for 'Constant dropping wears away stones,' and 'By diligence and patience the mouse ate through the cable,' and 'Little strokes fell great oaks.'

"Methinks I hear some of you say, 'Must a man afford himself no leisure? I will tell thee, my friend, what Poor Richard says, 'Employ thy time well, if thou meanest to gain leisure, and since thou art not sure of a minute, throw not away an hour.' Leisure is time for doing something useful; this leisure the diligent man will obtain, but the lazy man never, for a life of leisure and a life of laziness is two things. Many, without labour, would live by their wits only, but they break for want of stock, whereas industry gives comfort, and plenty, and respect. Fly pleasure, and they will follow you. 'The diligent spinner has a large swift; and now I have a sheep and a cow, everybody bids me good-morrow.'

"II. But without industry we must likewise be steady, settled and careful, and oversee our own affairs with our own eyes, and not trust too much to others; for, as Poor Richard says,

'I never saw an oft removed tree,
Nor yet an oft removed family,
That thrive as well as those that settled be.'

"And again, 'Three removes are as bad as a fire;' and again, 'Keep thy shop, and thy shop will keep thee;' and again, 'If you would have your business done, go, if not, send.' And again,

'He that by the plow would thrive.
Himself must either hold or drive.'

"And again, 'The eye of the master will do more work than both his hands;' and again, 'Want of care does us more damage than want of knowledge;' and again, 'Not to oversee workmen is to them your purse open.' Trusting too much to others' care is the ruin of many. For in the affairs of this world men are saved, not by faith, but by want of it, but a man's own care is profitable; for 'If you would have a faithful servant, and one that you like, serve yourself.' A little neglect may breed great mischief; 'for want of a nail the shoe was lost; for want of a shoe the horse was lost; for want of a horse the rider was lost, being overtaken and slain by the enemy.' All for want of a little care about a horse shoe nail.

"III. So much for industry, my friends, and attention to one's own business; but to these we must add frugality, if we would make our industry more certainly successful. A man may, if he knows not how to save as he gets, keep his nose all his life to the grindstone, and die not worth a groat at last. 'A fat kitchen makes a lean will;' and

'Many estates are spent in getting,
Since women for tea forsook spinning and knitting,
And men for punch forsook hewing and splitting.'

"If you would be wealthy, think of saving as well as of getting. The Indies have not made Spain rich, because her outgoes are greater than her incomes.

"Away, then, with your expensive follies, and you will not then have as much cause to complain of hard times, heavy taxes, and chargeable families. And farther, 'What maintains one vice would bring up two children.' You may think, perhaps, that a little tea or a little punch, now and then, can be no great matter, but remember, 'many a little makes a mickle.' Beware of little expenses; 'A small leak will sink a great ship,' as Poor Richard says; and again, 'Who dainties love, shall beggars prove,' and moreover, 'Fools make feasts and wise men eat them.'

"Here you are, all together at this sale of goods and knicknacks. You call them *goods*; but, if fineries you do not take care they will prove *evils* to some of you. You expect they will be sold cheap, and perhaps they may for less than the cost, but, if you have no occasion for them, they must be dear to you. Remember what Poor Richard says, 'Buy what thou hast no need of, and ere long thou shalt sell thy necessaries.' And again, 'At a great penny worth, pause a while.' He means that perhaps the cheapness is apparent only, and not real; or the bargain, by straightening thee in thy business, may do thee more harm than good. For in another place he says, 'Many have been ruined by buying good penny's worths. Again, 'It is foolish to lay out money in a purchase of repentance,' and yet this folly is practised every day at auction, for want of minding the almanac. Many a one, for the sake of finery on the back, have gone with a hungry belly and half starved their families. 'Silks and satins, scarlets and velvets, put the kitchen fires out,' as Poor Richard says.

"These are not the necessaries of life; they can scarcely be called the conveniences, and yet only because they look pretty, how many want to have them? By these and other extravagances, the genteel are reduced to poverty, and forced to borrow from those whom they formerly despised, but who, through industry and frugality, have maintained their standing, in which case it appears plainly that 'A ploughman on his legs is higher than a gentleman on his knees,' as Poor Richard says. Perhaps they have had a small estate left them, which they knew not the getting of; they think 'It is day and it will never be night,' that a little to be spent out of so much is not worth minding; but 'Always taking out of the meal tub and never putting in, soon comes to the bottom,' as Poor Richard says; and then, 'When the well is dry, they know the worth of water.' But this they might have known before if they had taken his advice. 'If you would know the value of money, go and try to borrow some, for he that goes a borrowing goes a sorrowing,' as Poor Richard says; and indeed so does he that lends to such people, when he goes to get it again. Poor Dick further advises and says,

'Fond pride of dress is sure a very curse,
Ere fancy you consult, consult your purse.'

And again, 'Pride is as loud a beggar as want, and a great deal more saucy.' When you have bought one fine thing, you must buy ten more, that your appearances may be all of a price; but Poor Dick says, 'It is easier to suppress the first desire than to satisfy all that follow it. And it is as truly folly for the poor to ape the rich, as for the frog to swell in order to equal the ox.'

'Vessels large may venture more,
But little boats should keep near shore.'

"It is, however, a folly soon punished, for as Poor Richard says, 'Pride that dines on vanity, sups on contempt. Pride breakfasted with plenty, dined with poverty and supped with infamy.' And after all, of what use is this pride of appearance, for which so much is risked, so much is suffered? It cannot promote health, nor ease pain; it makes no increase of merit in the person; it creates envy; it hastens misfortunes.

"But what madness must it be to *run in debt* for these superfluities? We are offered by the terms of this sale, six months' credit, and that, perhaps, has induced some of us to attend it, because we cannot spare the ready money, and hope now to be fine without it. But ah! think what you do when you run in debt; you give to another power over your liberty. If you cannot pay at the time, you will be ashamed to see your creditor, and will be in fear when you speak to him; you will make poor, pitiful, sneaking excuses, and, by degrees, come to lose your veracity, and sink into base, downright lying; for 'The second vice is lying, the first is running in debt,' as Poor Richard says, and again, to the same purpose, 'Lying rides on debt's back,' whereas a free born ought not to be ashamed, or afraid to see or speak to any man living. But poverty often deprives a man of all spirit and virtue. 'It is hard for an empty bag to stand upright.' What would you think of that prince or that government who should issue an edict forbidding you to dress like a gentleman or gentlewoman, on pain of imprisonment or servitude? Would you not say that you were free, have a right to dress as you please, and that such an edict would be a breach of privileges, and such a government tyrannical? And yet you are about to put yourself under such tyranny when you run in debt for such dress! Your creditor has authority at his pleasure to deprive you of your liberty, by confining you in jail till you shall be able to pay him. When you have got your bargain, you may, perhaps, think little of payment, but as Poor Richard says, 'Creditors have better memories than debtors; creditors are a superstitious set, great observers of set days and times.' The day comes round before you are aware, and the demand is made before you are prepared to satisfy it; or, if you bear your debt in mind, the time, which at first seemed so long, will, as it lessens, appear extremely short. Time will seem to have added wings to his heels as well as his shoulders. 'Those have a short Lent who owe money to be paid at Easter.' At present you may think yourselves in thriving circumstances, and that you can bear a little extravagance without injury, but

'For age and want save while you may—
No morning sun lasts a whole day.'

"Gain may be temporary and uncertain, but even while you live, expense is constant and certain. 'It is easier to build two chimneys than to keep one in fuel,' as Poor Richard says, so, 'Rather go to bed supperless than rise in debt.'

"IV. This doctrine, my friends, is reason and wisdom, but, after all, do not depend too much upon your industry, and frugality, and prudence, though excellent things, for they will all be blasted without the blessing of heaven, and therefore, ask that blessing humbly, and be not uncharitable to those that at present seem to want it, but comfort and help them. Remember, Job suffered, and was afterwards prosperous.

"And now to conclude,—'Experience keeps a dear school but fools will learn in no other,' as Poor Richard says, and scarce in that, for it is true, 'We may give advice, but we cannot give conduct.' However, remember this, 'They that will not be counselled cannot be helped;' and further, that 'If you will not hear Reason, she will rap your knuckles,' as Poor Richard says.

"Thus the old man ended his harangue. The people heard it and approved the doctrine, and immediately practised the contrary, just as if it had been a common sermon; for the auction opened, and they began to buy extravagantly. I found the good man had thoroughly studied my almanacs, and digested all I had dropped on these topics during the course of twenty-five years. The frequent mention he made of me must have tired any one else, but my vanity was wonderfully delighted with it, though I was conscious that not a tenth part of the wisdom was my own which he ascribed to me, but rather the gleanings that I had made of the sense of all ages and nations. However, I resolved to be the better for the echo of it, and, though I had at first determined to buy stuff for a new coat, I went away resolved to wear my old one a little longer. Reader, if thou wilt do the same, thy profit will be as good as mine.

"I am, as ever thine to serve thee,
      "RICHARD SANDERS."

For the Planter.

State Fair.

The State Fair at Petersburg was generally considered a successful and creditable affair. The intercourse of persons, strangers to each other personally, meeting together and discussing questions relating to agriculture, in which all are interested and engaged, has a happy tendency, and a good effect. We become acquainted with each other, with the diverse modes of doing business in different parts of our State, and thus often obtain new ideas in our own business, or may make new suggestions to others. One of the most valuable features of these annual gatherings, is the discussion carried on by the society at night, in which all are invited to give their experience in any thing relating to agriculture, whether it be an improved mode of operation in farming, new implements, or any thing bearing upon general cultivation. There is one great advantage, it appears to me, that might arise from these discussions that now does not obtain, and that is a good reporter to take them down, and then publish them with the society's transactions. In this way their benefit would be generally circulated, and be of advantage to others besides those present at these meetings. Many who desire it cannot attend them.

The "American Pomological Society" that lately met in New York City, have been in the practice of having their discussions on fruit, &c., reported, and published in their transactions. In this way a large amount of valuable information is disseminated yearly, and is of far more practical value than if merely confined to the members of the society then present. A like benefit would result to the public by having the discussions of the State Agricultural Society published also, and I would most respectfully suggest, that in future the Executive Committee be directed to employ a competent reporter to take them down, and that they be published in the transactions of the Society, even if the premiums should have to be lessened to provide for the expense.

I attended one of these discussions one evening in Petersburg, and was much interested with the subject of under-draining land, and the cultivation of corn, as spoken to by members then present. These discussions satisfied me that a more general acquaintance with the principles of geology would be desirable. We have in our State, and often in a small part of it, all the members of the geological columns, and in many parts of the State they are largely developed. The tertiary deposits for instance, cover most of the State from the head of tide-water to the ocean, and here its beds of "sand and gravel, of clay, marl and shells, are every where to be seen, and a knowledge of their position and extent would be of invaluable advantage in underdraining such lands. Though not personally acquainted with much of that region of country, there is reason to believe that the higher grounds between the rivers and large streams, in general, has a sandy and gravelly soil, and

that this stratum often, if not generally, extends beneath the vallies, and that there a bed of clayey or loamy soil rests atop of it. This upper stratum often contains a sufficiency of clay to make it difficult for surface-water to penetrate beneath it, and the surface being nearly level, causes the water to be retained to the injury of growing crops. This bed of sand and gravel often comes to the surface on higher ground, and the water there entering it, it becomes saturated beneath the bed of clay, causing the water there to press upward, and where it can issue, will cause a spring at the surface, but more generally will ooze very gradually through the clay bed and make the surface a cold and wet soil, unfavorable to grain crops. This appears to have been the condition of the lands of the President on Pamunky River, which he had drained very effectually by tapping this bed of gravel at the lowest possible point by a deep ditch, thus drawing off the water from the gravel bed, and preventing its pressure upward through the more compact bed above it, and thus draining land at least half a mile off.

Another member gave his experience in underdraining, where the stratum was similar with but this difference, the under bed of sand and gravel, instead of being saturated with water, was comparatively dry. Here this bed evidently had an outlet on lower ground, perhaps in the bed of a river, and thus was drained off its water. Here an opposite course of operation answered the end effectually. As it was only necessary to guard against surface water, this was done by boring holes with a post-auger through the clay bed into the gravel bed, thus discharging the surface water in that way. This being done in the lowest places, and when the field was put down to wheat, and the holes left open, would protect that crop. Stones not being convenient, else the holes might have been filled with them; but as they were renewed with little labor, they could be easily opened again at the sowing of the next crop, when stock would not be admitted in the field. These holes would partially fill up during winter, but answered the end effectually for the time.

Here were two distinct operations for draining land, both answering the purpose under their respective conditions, and it is not unlikely both might be adopted to advantage in some localities. For instance, where the gravel bed could be drained as the President's was, there might be places where the surface water could be more readily discharged by boring post-holes into the gravel bed than by any other mode.

Other modes of underdraining were practised by other persons. These different plans show the necessity of studying the character of the formations beneath the surface, so as to adopt the best method of effecting the end desired. In other parts of the State these plans could not be carried out. In the Piedmont region of our State, bordering the Blue Ridge, we have no beds of sand and gravel, or of clay, lying horizontally beneath the surface. Our soil is derived entirely from the decomposition of the primitive rocks now in place, and they being tilted up at a high angle, presents the different strata of rocks, either wholly or partially decomposed in that situation. And these strata being full of cracks, seams, and fissures, readily admit the water into the bowels of our hills, from whence it finds its way out to the surface of the foot of the hills in small streams, giving us an abundance of good water for stock purposes. No other country with which I am acquainted is as well watered as this. Many farms may be divided into ten acre fields, and have running water in every field, and yet but little land that needs underdraining—the country is too rolling for surface water to lie long on the ground. Some few spots are benefitted by being thrown into beds, as is practised largely on tide-water.

Some discussion on the cultivation of corn was incidentally entered into, and some questions asked whether deep cultivation of growing corn was best, and whether hilling it up was advisable. Experience is the best test in this matter, and I propose to state the mode adopted by one of my sons, who now farms my land. His plan is, to plough deeply—in the spring if possible—as soon as the ground is in good order after the frost is out of it. There is always a longer, or shorter season, at that time, when the ground is in good order for ploughing mellow. This is preferred to fall ploughing. Then, at the proper season, harrow the ground to a fine tilth, but be sure *to do that*, by using the clod-crusher if not effected without it. He has made an implement to mark his ground—in this way. He takes the fore-wheels, axle, and tongue, of Pitt's Thresher and Cleaner, and to these he has attached a piece of timber, say four inches square and longer than the width of two rows of corn, with three arms about two or three feet long mortised into it, and fastened to the axle at each end, and the middle with a hinge-joint, so as to raise up and down. Into this piece of timber are three other pieces mortised, say two feet long, to stand at an angle like a shovel plough stock; to these pieces, small shovels are attached and placed just as far apart as we want the rows of corn to be. Then with one hand and two horses, three rows may be marked out at a time, thus doing work rapidly; go over the field both ways before planting, then drop the corn cross-ways of the last marking out—it will be much more correctly dropped than to go the other way.

For covering the corn he uses horse power, with a plough somewhat similar to a shovel plough, only with two shovels fastened to the stock of the plough by a bar of iron bent in form of a half circle with a small shovel at each end about one foot apart, and the middle of the plough attached to the plough stock. Thus by running one shovel on each side of dropped corn, it is covered with a small ridge over it; this ridge will not bake so hard with heavy rains as if covered flat, and the corn comes up better; and then if we have heavy, washing rains, the shovel marks on each side of the row leads the water along side the corn, and not over it, and prevents its washing as badly as if the whole of the water ran over the hill of corn. This advantage was very perceptible in this section last spring with our heavy rains, the corn was not washed, I suppose, half as badly as if the old mode of planting had been adopted. This places the corn but little below the level of the ground, and if the ground is in proper order, it is hardly necessary to again harrow it, but after the corn gets up a little, run a double-shovel pretty close to the corn, so as to throw a little earth around the hill, then after the grass and weeds begin to grow again, go through it the other way, covering up the grass around the hills, in the meanwhile thin it at suitable times, and use such fertilizers as may be advisable. We have seldom used any thing but plaster and ashes, and never put a hoe into the corn field after planting, if then. We very often go through our corn but twice to cultivate, sometimes, though rarely, three times, and with fair seasons we expect from 40 to 60 bushels per acre. We then decidedly prefer level culture, using only double-shovels, and they not large ones—and deprecate hilling of corn in cultivation, or stirring the ground deeply after planting. The ground can be much easier put in order before planting than after, and then the after work is much easier.   YARDLEY TAYLOR.

Loudon Coun'y.

For the Planter.

The Guano Controversy.

MR. EDITOR—I am "old fogy" enough still to think that true faith and sound principles are necessary in order to good morals and correct practice. In the August number of the Planter, over the signature of "Wm. A. Bradford," I was pleased to find a well written piece, which ably supports my views as set forth in a critique upon "X. of the Republican," and in my replication to his rejoinder, to wit: that guano is not a mere stimulant, furnishing no pabulum for the plant, nor fertility to the soil. This is ably sustained by Mr. Bradford; but *he* denies what *I* admitted, that guano and other manuring agents, *may "stimulate"* the plant. Says that gentleman: "I do apprehend how in the animal kingdom agencies of this kind (meaning stimulants) are more or less operative, but I have yet to learn the mode in which the vegetable kingdom is rendered thus impressible." Now, sir, it is plainly one thing to know the fact of a certain existence, and quite another to "apprehend" the mode and manner of its existence and operation. We *know* that food, taken into a healthy stomach, nourishes the body, but how the process of digestion, assimulation and final appropriation to fat, muscle, bone, sinew, &c., is carried on, has not been, and may never be "apprehended" by finite minds. The thing to be apprehended, is not "the mode in which the vegetable kingdom is rendered thus impressible," but the fact. If the fact is found to exist—there must be some "mode," whether "apprehended" or not. Again says this gentleman, "vegetables are not subject to the action of mere stimulants. In its common acceptation, a stimulant is any agent that exalts or quickens the vital forces or actions." Animals that have to seek their food, are endowed with sensation and are urged by the calls of nature, to use the powers of locomotion with which they are constituted, to meet the de-

mands of appetite, but the poor plant feels no want of food, and if it did, it is incapable of making any exertion to obtain it."— Some animals have "no power of locomotion," and will scarcely be "urged by the calls of nature" to use powers of locomotion with which they are "not" constituted.— What then? Of course having no use for it, they have no "sensation," and cannot be "subject to the action of mere stimulants." Thus it may be seen the gentleman places some animals and vegetables in the same category. Where then shall the stand point be found, above which the susceptibility to stimulants ranges, and below which it ceases. Animals have "powers of locomotion" to seek food, and are therefore "endowed with sensation." "Vegetables" have no "powers of locomotion," and therefore *they* have no sensation. But some *animals* have no "powers of locomotion," and therefore they too have no sensation. Is not this a logical sequence? Again, "vegetables," says the same writer, "are destitute of the semblance of nervous excitability." If this be true, how is it that the sun-flower inclines to the sun in his diurnal course? Will the answer be, because it has been thus constituted?— This explains no more than to say, *it is so because it is so.* Why may we not say that the "vegetable" being "endowed" with "excitability, or the susceptibility of being acted upon by the rays of the sun, thus inclines? How is it that the leaves of the sensative plant droop upon a touch of the hand? that some flowers close their petals upon a similar touch, and some again are open by day and close at night? These are facts, and demonstrate that "vegetables are rendered thus impressible." The gentleman admits plants to be "provided with organs of circulation, absorption and secretion," and that these organs are controlled by physical laws and though destitute of the rudest form of nerves, yet that there exists a mysterious force, a *vis vitæ*—a "divinity within that shapes its end." All this I contend but demonstrates that "they are thus impressible" and are susceptible of "the action of stimulants," agents that exalt and quickens the vital forces or actions." Vitality is indeed dormant, without the action of such agents, and can exhibit none of the active properties or phenomena of life. The leafless tree and torpid toad present like spectacles, in the animal and vegetable kingdoms. The genial warmth of the vernal sun awakens (stimulates) each to life again. "But how it exists, or where the force resides," is, very truly, "beyond human ken," as all the operations of nature are. "For who by searching can find out God?"

One remark more: The gentleman seems to ascribe the difference in the permanence of guano as a manure, and the ordinary home-made manures, entirely to the larger quantity of such manures as commonly applied. This may, to some *small* extent, be true—but I think it ascribable to a much greater extent, to the fact, that all home-made manures contain a large proportion of coarse material, that cannot be elaborated and assimilated, to a condition to act as food for the plant sooner than the second or even the third year after its application, whereas guano is already in a state to meet the demands of the plant, needing only due mixture with soil and solution.

Notwithstanding this liberty of criticism has been taken, I render to the gentleman a tribute of thanks, that he has rendered me such timely and efficient aid in my conflict with the Herculean lance of "X. of the Republican." Should his shot overtake "X." prancing on his gallant hobby, "stimulate the soil," it can scarcely fail to inflict a fatal wound.　　　　　B.

For the Southern Planter.

Action of Lime and Marl on Tide-Water Soils.

The October number of the Southern Planter contains an article from "Wm. D. Gresham, Esq., of Forest Hill, King & Queen county," entitled the "Action of Lime, or Marl, on Soils Below the Falls of the Tide-Water Rivers of Virginia." All he says of both lime and marl is true, and but for them our Tide-Water country would have been abandoned by its owners, as it begun to be in 1832, and as it continued to be for several years thereafter. But the emigrants to the "Sunny South," encountering unlooked for privations and sacrifices, had cause to long for the "flesh pots" of Old Virginia, and to observe that the few who remained at home, and bought themselves rich by buying their lands at from three and a half to four dollars the acre, were doing a better business than they who were "going out" to make cotton. About this time, or a little after, the "Farmer's Register" was commenced in "little Petersburg," by Edmund Ruffin, Esq., and much did it do to keep men here at home, and to stop the Southern and South-Western tide then "setting in." About that time a distant light first began to gleam upon the vision of our most intelligent farmers.

From pride, birth, and the ownership of estates that none save the Indians and their own cavalier ancestors ever owned, the present owners did not wish to sell. This determined them to find some means to enable them to hold these lands—when lo! the lands themselves contained the means within them. A little research, a little exertion, deep drainage, and the application of lime or marl, transformed these "old fields" into prairies; the forlorn homestead into a tasty mansion, that a Davis or a Percivall might have fashioned. Lands purchased from spendthrift owners in 1843, at $17, in 1858 are worth more than $60 per acre. Such is the "action of lime or marl on soils below the falls of the Tide-Water Rivers of Virginia," yet, all is not known nor understood. These miocene marls *most always* betoken the proximity of eocene marl. The converse, however, is *not* true. Miocene is the top, eocene the bottom. We have the bottom along our rivers, without the top, but never the top without the bottom, because it is too weighty. Understand me. The eocene is not necessarily immediately under the miocene, but it is not far off. I have seen them in close proximity. But whoever, in the Pamunkey country, has miocene marl, will find the eocene if he will but look for it. In the cliffs and ravines where he finds his miocene, if he will go low enough, he will be certain of reaching eocene. This I have seen both from farming experience and from cuttings on the York River Railroad. I expect it is equally true of the Mattapony country. For on one occasion I remember to have seen eocene marl in the river bank just above Mantua, and on another occasion in Gloucester, at Warner Hall, I saw what I took for eocene marl, but the owner said it was miocene marl and marsh mud combined, (what is called in this county "blue fuller.") It is a rich marl, but to which class it belongs I am not geologist enough to say, though I am farmer enough to have used it, and to have found it a *rapid* improver. I applied it on forty acres of land, which had made previous to its application but two barrels and a half of corn per acre, and this year, dry as it has been, it made five barrels of corn per acre. We do not altogether know what we possess in this lower country, beyond the certainty of ague and fever, which deep drainage and a free use of lime or marl will remedy, and in some cases prevent.

Tide-Water farmers, who would not check their career of improvement, must beware of *tobacco*, lest while they are making that, to obtain cash in hand, their capital is depreciating. For the $100 per acre to be made on twenty acres of tobacco, they are losing $40 per acre on the hundred acres of land they might marl whilst making the twenty acres of tobacco. Land worth twenty dollars per acre down here, having three hundred bushels of eocene marl per acre applied to it, is immediately worth forty dollars per acre. The more heavily you marl within a reasonable limit, and the more deeply you drain, the more heavily you can crop. We present the singular phenomenon of owning land which we can crop "*ad infinitum*," and improve "*ad infinitum*," at the same time, and under the same process. Tobacco, however, is a crop demanding so much attention and care, that whilst that care and attention are being bestowed on it, the rest of the farm is being neglected. If gentlemen would first get their lands heavily marled, and deeply drained, they may then entertain tobacco speculations with propriety, for then "with the will there comes the way," and not until then. With proper care and attention we can raise any product of the temperate zone. This, all may not believe, but it is nevertheless true. We want our farmers to be educated, and we want capital to come amongst us. I have never yet known a well educated man, with a tolerable command of capital, who once located amongst us, who wanted to quit. In ease and cheapness of access to market, and the number of markets open and available to us, no country can excel ours. All of these are matters of the first moment, and the larger our Atlantic cities grow, and the more numerous they become, the greater must be their influence on the price of all lands tributary to them by means of steam and sail navigation. Who was the first Tide-Water man, who commenced the use of marl, I cannot say, I have *heard* that old Mr. John Roane, of King William, was the first. He marled a lot and was so pleased at the result, that he never failed to take his visitors to see it, but *never* marled *any more.*

(I won't sware to the truth of this.) Next was Mr. Thomas Carter, of Pampatike. He marled his front field, but so heavily that it is only within the last few years that the land has recovered from the excessive application. Both of these were miocene marls. After that, the use of eocene marl was commenced on a farm in King William county, not far from Newcastle Ferry, (but not the Newcastle farm,) and the friends of this gentleman feared that a love of good society, and of eocene marl, *would break him.* This was as far back as 1833. What induced the three gentlemen above named to use these marles I cannot say, but have a vague impression that they had been used in New Jersey under the direction of Professor Henry D. Rodgers, who, from geological information, and from the use of marls in England, advised their use in New Jersey, and wherever *else* they were known to exist. I cannot tell the exact year the "Farmer's Register" was begun, but think the gentlemen above mentioned had commenced their experiments *prior* to its publication. That Journal took the matter up, and did all it could to encourage the use of both lime and marl. If any one who may read this has information as to who was *certainly* the *first* man to use marl, and *what induced* its use, we will be much pleased to learn. The reader must not understand me as saying, that the mere fact of owning a farm with marl under it, is synonymous with having a rich one. The poorest farm I now can think of, is one with the greatest amount of natural advantages. It is enterprise and exertion, combined with a vigorous attention, that changes the Pamunky and its adjacent sand-fields, into

"Sweet fields arrayed in living green, and
  rivers of delight."

On these same sands and marshes, where once the partridge and the snipe were the best owners, now are seen "a most living landscape, and the wave of woods and corn-fields, and the abodes of men scattered at intervals, and wreathing smoke arising from such rustic roofs." The whistle of the farm steam engine, and the creak of the marl cart, all tell the age and section in which we live. I, for one, believe that Eastern Virginia has seen her lowest ebb, and that the "springs of the rising tide" will bear us on to greatness. With the "Enquirer" of *old,* let us say "*nous verrons.*"

TIDE-WATER FARMER.

From the Michigan Farmer.

The Feeding of Milk Cattle.

If a Farmer have a pair of cattle, and he neither wants them to work nor to make beef, he feeds them enough to keep them in condition, but whenever he wants them for a long pull of steady work, he begins to give them food in quantities that will not only support them, but will also supply all that they waste by muscular exertion. If he does not feed in that way the cattle will not only lose flesh, but at last will become so weak that they cannot perform a full day's work, so that the farmer suffers pecuniarily in two ways by this attempt at being saving—for the cattle decrease in value, and their work is also less in amount than it should be. Every farmer will exclaim, "The man who does business in that way, is unwise, and imprudent, as well as ignorant of his true interests;" yet it is very probable, that the same process of depreciation is going on in their own barn-yards amongst their milch cows.

What is milk? Is it not a certain amount of raw material, produced by the animal either from a surplus of food, or by a waste of the actual substance of the body. If the animal has a surplus of food *and is able to consume it*, its body suffers no diminution, nor does the supply of milk; but when it has only a sufficiency of food to support the waste constantly going on from vital action, the supply of milk is only yielded at the expense of the carcase, and the farmer loses at both ends, the cows depreciating in value, and the yield of milk being less and less, until it is utterly dried off, and there is nothing left but a skin and a skeleton.

It is no unusual incident to have a farmer point out to us one of these specimens of skin and skeleton as the best cow he has in his yard for milk, with the remark that, "she is a splendid cow when she is in flesh, or before calving, but that as soon as she calves, she runs all to milk, and becomes as poor as a crow." Now the fact is that the cow is really a valuable animal probably, and is willing to do all that can be asked to be profitable. She has large organs for secreting milk, which will act while ever there is anything left for them to work upon, and when the food does not supply it, they draw upon the body. Such a cow as that is not rightly fed, hence the reason she becomes thin and loses flesh after calving. Her milk secreting organs are not supplied with all the material which they can use, and the consequence is that they use up the cow. Let us look at the speed with which they use it?

A cow that will weigh 800 pounds, ought to consume about 20 pounds of the best hay per diem to keep her so that she will neither gain nor lose, supposing she gives no milk, nor does any kind of work whatever. Now a cow that gives ten quarts of milk per day, it is evident, ought to have enough food over and above that, *of the right kind*, to enable her to furnish that quantity of milk. What is the food which will do that? The composition of the milk will tell. Milk, according to the analysis of Haidlen, which is the best known, contains in 1000 parts:

Water	873.00
Butter	30.00
Casein	48.20
Milk Sugar	43.90
Phospate of Lime	2.31
Mineral Matters	2.59
	1000.00

So that in 10 quarts or 20 pounds of milk we would have of solid matter, 2.60, which would be composed as follows:

Butter	0.625	lbs.
Casein	1.000	"
Milk Sugar	0.875	"
Phosphate of Lime	0.045	"
Mineral Matters	0.055	"
	2.6	

In addition therefore to the 20 pounds of hay, there should be fed to the cow, substances containing from 25 to 30 per cent. of materials which will easily form the above elements, and which also will be so palatable that she will be induced to consume them readily. As an instance of the truth of this, we give the result of an experiment made with three cows which calved about the same time, and were each treated differently.

No. 1. On the 1st of January or about three weeks after calving, gave 15½ quarts of milk per day, and weighed 980 pounds She was fed 28 pounds of hay per day, and in nine weeks lost 84 pounds of flesh, and fell off to 9½ quarts of milk per day.

No. 2. At the same date gave 12 quarts, and weighed 840 pounds. She was fed 18 pounds of hay 45 pounds of turnips, and 9 pounds of ground oats for four weeks, when the ration of ground oats was discontinued.

Then she lost in both flesh and milk, and at the end of nine weeks, she lost 28 pounds of flesh, and gave but 6¼ quarts of milk.

No. 3. Gave 15½ quarts of milk per day and weighed 1092 pounds. She was fed, with a steamed mixture of cut hay and straw, oat chaff, turnips, bran, meal and rape cake, which actually cost less than the feed of No. 2, by about 20 cents for the nine weeks. At the end of the trial she had gained in flesh 56 pounds, and her milk averaged 12½ quarts per day.

To keep a cow fully up to her milk, rating it at 10 quarts per day, it has been estimated, that it would need over and above the amount of hay required for her necessary maintenance, 10 lbs. of hay to supply the casein, and 20 lbs. to yield the oleaginous elements for the butter, and 4½ lbs. for the supply of the phosphoric acid and other minerals. No cow could eat hay enough to supply the amount, and therefore, if we would have them fully profitable, they must be fed on other materials. It must be borne in mind also, that where butter is the manufactured article, the substances used may very much promote a supply of milk yielding a large proportion of butter.

So convinced was an English gentleman, named Horsfall, of this fact, and of the importance of keeping up his milch cows in flesh, so that he might not lose, after calving, the flesh which they had made previous to that time, that he instituted a number of experiments, and found that when his milch cows were kept up in flesh, their cream was worth nearly twice as much as that yielded by ordinary milk for the purposes of making butter.

For instance, good milk of more than ordinary quality will seldom yield over one ounce of butter to a quart of milk, and when the cream is taken, the richest known yield is at the rate of 14 ounces of butter to a quart of cream, but more generally it seldom exceeds 9 or 10 ounces to the quart. Mr. Horsfall found that by his mode of feeding, his cream would yield from a quart from 22 to 25 ounces of butter, and from the milk he got at the rate of 25 ounces of butter to every 40 pounds.

To obtain such results, however, Mr. Horsfall, found that he must feed his cows on food that besides sustaining the animal, would also contain a surplus of the elements of curd, of butter, and of bone, sufficient for the formation of the quantity of milk which the cow was in the habit of giving, or in other words the rations of food must contain casein, olein and phosphates, not only sufficient to supply the natural waste of the animal, by keeping up its muscles, its bones and its respiration, but also to enable it to give milk to the utmost powers of its secreting organs, fully saturated with the particles of butter.

He found that a cow could not possibly consume, were she to keep her jaws moving for the whole twenty-four hours, a quantity of either hay or turnips sufficient to produce milk or butter in such amount as would render the keeping of cows profitable, and that he must rely upon other articles of food, in the composition of which there were the requisite elements.

After various trials of different substances and mixtures, it was found that one of the most economical compounds, with regard to results, and value of the materials, was formed from rape cake, 5 pounds, bran 2 pounds, for each cow, mixed with a sufficient quantity of cut bean straw, and oat chaff, to supply each animal with three meals of as much as it would eat. This mixture was steamed, and with it was fed likewise, a pound of bean meal, 25 pounds of turnips or mangle wurzels and after each meal 4 pounds of hay.

The bean straw mentioned above, it may be well to note, is not the stalks of our field beans, but of the variety known as the Windsor bean. When dry, this straw is about as palatable as buckwheat straw, but when steamed " it becomes soft and pulpy, emits an agreeable odor, and imparts flavor and relish to the mess." It is not by any means equal to our corn stalks as a substance for feed, and we believe were corn stalks treated in the same way, they would prove more valuable. The rape cake used, is the remains of the seed of the cole wort or rape plant after it is pressed for its oil. The cole or rape plant is a vegetable of the turnip species, the seed of which is very rich in oils. The oil made from this seed is principally used for burning, and contains a large proportion of this fatty matter, as much as 10 per cent., besides nearly 40 per cent. more of starch, sugar and gum, all of which yield 50 parts of fat to every 90.

Heifers fed in this way, not giving milk, and dry cows intended for the butcher, increased fourteen pounds each per week, and sometimes even more, or at the rate of two pounds per day.

If we compare this kind of feeding with the treatment our milk cattle usually get during the winter, we will easily perceive the profit of one system and the want of profit in the other.

A milch cow that receives 20 pounds of the poorest quality of hay, and 8 quarts of bran per day, is considered as very well taken care of, not one half the cows in this State receive as much. Such hay is worth $6 per ton, and the bran is now sold at $8 per ton; it is therefore easy to calculate the cost of keeping a cow as being worth about eight cents per day, for the hay feeding is worth six cents and the bran estimated as averaging half a pound to the quart is worth nearly two cents. In return, the cow yields probably from four to six quarts of milk per day. Take the largest amount, and allowing each quart of milk to yield an ounce of butter, and we have as the daily return of the cow, 6 ozs. of butter, which at eighteen cents per pound, is worth 6¾ cts., exactly. The manure, and the skim milk, we allow as paying for the work of feeding, and the labor of manufacturing the butter. There would be a loss therefore on each cow of 1¼ cent per day, which in a dairy of six cows, kept at this rate, and averaging this amount of produce, for a whole winter, of 160 days, would amount to twelve dollars. We think this a moderate computation, and that the loss more generally reaches twice that amount, especially when it is considered that there is hardly a dairy in the State in which there are six cows that will average four quarts apiece per day for the whole of the winter, even on a better supply of food than that above noted.

In illustration of an extraordinary instance of feeding, and its profits, we give the following from a letter we received from Mr. Becket Chapman, of South Boston, Ionia County:

"In the winter of 1856, I fed one cow one and a half bushels of Indian meal and one and a half bushels of bran per week, besides what hay she would eat. She made eight pounds of butter per week. Corn was worth fifty cents per bushel, and bran 50 cents per 100 lbs. Butter sold at 25 cents.

"In the winter of 1857, I fed a cow six quarts of Indian meal scalded per day, with good hay *ad libitum*, good stable and plenty of litter. She made 10 lbs of butter per week. Corn was worth 75 cents per bushel, and butter 25 cents per pound. Will the editor please let us know if corn can be used to more advantage?"

We regret that Mr. Chapman has not given us some idea of the weight and value of hay he fed to his cows, but calling it 16 pounds per day, and worth $8 per ton, and we have the result per week as follows:

FIRST YEAR.

Hay, 112 lbs. at $8 per ton,................	$0.45
Corn Meal at 50 cts. per bushel for corn,..	0.90
Bran at 50 cts. per 100 lbs.,...............	0.25
	$1.60
Butter made 8 lbs. at 25 cts.,.............	2.00
Leaving as a profit per week,............	.40

SECOND YEAR.

Hay, 20 lbs. per day at $8 per ton,.......	$0.56
Indian Meal, 42 quarts, corn at 75 cts.,....	1.13
	$1.69
Produce, 10 lbs. of butter per week at 25 cts.,	2.50
Profit per week,........................	$0.81

It will be noted that after allowing four pounds of hay per day to make up for the want of the bran, the scalding of the meal seems to give a profit of 81 cents plus the increased price of the corn and the value of the six quarts saved, making altogether a difference of 88 cents in favor of the cooked food, and valuing the feed at the same rates as those of the year before, a profit per week of $1.18 from a single cow.

Though we do not think this the most profitable mode of feeding milk cows, yet, it is a fair illustration of the fact that cows will pay better to be kept right, than to have them uncared for and only half fed up to their work.

We call the attention of the butter-makers, and the keepers of milk stock to the facts set down here as worth their consideration. If any of them do better, and we have understated or underrated, any part of the subject, we are open for correction. Let the farmers give us facts, facts that come from the weighing beam,—we shall be pleased to receive them, the earlier the better as we shall have more to say on this subject.

Virginia State Agricultural Society.
SEVENTH ANNUAL MEETING.

Agreeably to the adjournment of the last Farmers' Assembly, a meeting of members elect for the present year assembled at the Market Street Baptist Church, in the city of Petersburg, on Monday Afternoon, the 1st of November, 1858.

It being manifest that no quorum was present, the meeting adjourned until Tuesday, the 2nd instant, at half-past 4 o'clock, P. M.

—

TUESDAY, Nov. 2nd, 1858.

At half past four o'clock the meeting assembled at the same place. The Secretary of the Virginia State Agricultural Society called the meeting to order, and proceeded to call the roll to ascertain whether or not a quorum was in attendance. Forty-four members were found to be present, sixty-five being necessary to constitute a quorum, the meeting again adjourned to half-past seven o'clock, P. M.

—

At half-past seven o'clock the Secretary again called the meeting to order, and proceeded as heretofore to ascertain the number in attendance, when the calling of the roll was arrested by a motion made, and put to the vote of the meeting by Mr. Cox, of Chesterfield, by which vote Col. Thomas M. Bondurant was elected Chairman of the meeting *pro tempore*. The Secretary of the Society was then requested to act as Clerk. The calling of the roll was resumed, and it appearing that but forty-five members were present, the meeting adjourned until Wednesday morning, 9 o'clock.

—

WEDNESDAY, Nov. 3rd, 1858.

The meeting assembled agreeably to adjournment, Col. Bondurant in the Chair.

Mr. Wickham, of Hanover, offered the following resolution :

Resolved, That the Farmers' Assembly is now in Session.

Pending the discussion on this resolution, on the motion of Mr. Booth, of Nottoway, the meeting adjourned until half-past seven o'clock this evening.

—

At half-past seven o'clock the meeting again assembled, Col. Bondurant in the Chair.

The resolution of Mr. Wickham, of Hanover, being the first business in order, was taken up, when, on motion of Mr. Garnett, of Westmoreland, it was laid upon the table. Mr. Garnett then moved the adoption of the following resolution, which was carried in the affirmative :

Resolved, That the Secretary do now proceed to call the roll, to ascertain whether there be a quorum present, of the Farmers' Assembly.

The roll was accordingly called, and there being found present but forty-five members, it was, on motion,

Resolved, That this meeting do now adjourn *sine die*.

—

After the final adjournment of the meeting, the Secretary distributed among the members elect the following annual report of the Executive Committee to the Farmers' Assembly, with the accompanying documents, which, through the courtesy and respect due to the Assembly, had been withheld, so long as there remained a hope of effecting an organization .

ANNUAL REPORT OF THE PRESIDENT AND EXECUTIVE COMMITTEE.

Members of the Farmers Assembly :

At your last session, in 1857, and by your several special orders sundry duties were entrusted to the Executive Committee, and which were thus required to be finally decided upon and completed by that Committee. What has been done, or failed to be effected in these cases will be first presented to your notice.

The President and Executive Committee, in their last Annual Report, had referred to the heavy expenditures attending the Society's exhibitions as a growing evil, and to the efforts then made to restrain them. The partial success of those efforts may be seen on reference to the accompanying document, (A.)

The policy of holding our Fairs at Richmond, upon an advance by the City, of an inadequate sum of money, had drawn so heavily upon the contingent or surplus fund of the Society, that if we had held the present Fair there, that surplus fund amounting originally to about $5,000, which was reduced in 1857 to $3,000, would have been entirely exhausted, and, in addition, a debt incurred which could only have been paid out of the fixed capital of the Society.

The first clause of the 11th section of the Constitution provides that, "All capital of the Society, now or hereafter invested, shall be held a fund sacred to the cause of Agricultural improvement, of which the income only shall be subject to appropriation."

This made it imperative upon the Executive Committee to procure from the City, or citizens, of Richmond, an adequate guarantee that the expenditures for holding the present Fair should not exceed the income subject to appropriation, and that the accommodations therefor should be commodious and in proper repair. And as the Constitution requires that "The Society shall hold an Annual Exhibition, Cattle Show and Fair, at such time and place as the Farmers Assembly shall designate, or in default thereof as may be designated by the Executive Committee," the President and Executive Committee brought their difficulties to the attention of the Farmers Assembly, in the following passage in their last Annual Report: "The ground allowed to the Society for the Annual Fair and Exhibition, is insufficient in space and accommodations. The Executive Committee, for the last two years have encountered much difficulty to make up for the actual deficiencies—and in vain efforts to obtain a suitable and permanent location. On this account also, the expenses of the Society have been much increased. It is absolutely necessary that these disadvantages shall be removed, by some proper and permanent arrangement, in the ensuing year, even if a necessary condition for relief shall be a removal of the Fair to some other location, either neighboring or remote." As the Constitution devolved on the Farmers Assembly the duty of designating a place for the Annual Fair, and in default thereof made it the business of the Executive Committee to supply their omission, it was earnestly hoped that this responsibility would have been taken by the Farmers Assembly. The subject was referred to a special committee of that body, who asked to be discharged from its further consideration, and that it should be referred back to the Executive Committee. This course was adopted by the Farmers Assembly, and left the Executive Committee no alternative but to raise the necessary funds in Richmond, or to appeal to the liberality of some other city. The accompanying document (B) will show what the Executive Committee considered it their duty to do under these circumstances. From that, it will appear that the City of Richmond declined to render such aid as the Executive Committee felt compelled to require, whilst the City of Petersburg, under the lead of the Union Society, of Virginia and North Carolina, proposed terms whose generosity entitles them to the thanks of the Virginia State Agricultural Society. These terms, as is apparent, were accepted; and the Society is accordingly convened in Petersburg.

If this change of locality is to be the commencement of a new system as to the terms on which the Fairs of the Society are to be held, it has at least one advantage in the precedent it affords, by which it shall be a fixed condition that the city or town having the benefit of the Fair will contribute an amount sufficient to enable the Society to hold it without violating the provisions of the Constitution.

Having thus concisely stated the grounds of their action, which are hereby respectfully submitted to the Farmers Assembly, the Executive Committee will cheerfully receive their instructions as to any further action upon the subject.

Acting under either the special or virtual instructions of the Farmers Assembly, and in continuation of the still earlier adopted and continued policy of the State Agricultural Society, the Executive Committee endeavored to obtain from the General Assembly of the Commonwealth, the enactment of several measures required for the improvement and profit of agriculture, and for the removal of existing burdens and grievances. Among these, the principal objects sought, were, pecuniary aid to the State Society—relief from the worst, and only the useless as well as oppressive features of the general fence law (and so far only in the main respects, as to be sought for and accepted by voluntary agreement in particular neighbourhoods,)—and relief from the inspections of manures, which are taxes on agriculture and of no benefit whatever except to supply fees to the inspectors. Neither of these measures of benefit or relief to agriculture has ever been fully considered or finally determined upon by the Legislature.

The subject of the offer to the Society by Col. Philip St. George Cocke, of the Belona Arsenal property at the price with interest at which he had bought it, on the condition of there being established there by the Society an Agricultural Institute, or school, was referred by your body to the Executive Committee and was promptly and deliberately considered and acted upon. The reasons of the Committee for declining the offer are set forth in the accompanying abstract (C) from the Journal of the Executive Committee.

The expenditures of the last year, (1857) not known or nearly completed at the time of the last Annual Report, though still much too large, are considerably curtailed in their total amount by different measures of improved economy. Yet, in the expenditures for that year, was included, the amount paid for printing the transactions of the Society, which before had been two years in arrear, and bringing the publication up to the latest time—which is now the established policy. But with all the attempts made to reduce expenses, still, (as shown in the papers A and B.,) the expenses of the year and Fair of 1857, much exceeded the income and receipts of the Society— as the expenses of 1858 would have done, but for the change of location and of the system. Thus it has been, and would have continued, that the expenses of the Annual Fairs, added to other minor and indispensable expenditures, would have been more than enough to absorb all the income and available means of the Society, leaving, as heretofore, not a dollar to devote to any other mode of increasing agricultural knowledge, or promoting agricultural interests. In that case, all that has yet been done, or could be done, by fairs alone, would be but a poor result from its means. We would be among the last to depreciate the very important utility and benefits of great agricultural fairs, and the crowds of visitors attracted to them, consisting of the best population of our country. We would not abate a word of what was said in the last Annual Report, in eulogizing the social and general benefits of such fairs and meetings as this Society has heretofore held. But highly valuable as such fairs are—and more so for their indirect and remote benefits than for their direct and immediate influence on agriculture, yet it is very certain, that the holding of fairs and exhibitions is neither the only nor the most effective means, by which our Society can, with its funds, promote instruction in, and the improvement and progress of agriculture. And should it be a necessary result of removal to different, or even always changing localities for the Annual Fairs, and the requiring that the fairs shall defray their proper expenses, that their particular benefits shall be greatly reduced, such change will at least leave the Society free, and able, to devote its income, so released, to the amount of some $3,000 annually, to other measures for aiding agricultural instruction and improvement. There are many such measures that might be judiciously and profitably put in action. Without designing to indicate any of these as the best, or deserving the earliest preference, we will refer, in general terms, to two only of such measures, both of unquestionable utility, if judiciously planned and executed, and either of which might be so extended as to absorb most beneficially for agriculture, much more than all that this Society can thus be enabled to pay for any such objects.

One of the measures referred to, is one which has already much engaged the attention and interest of the Society, and which was first brought forward in the General meeting of 1854, and discussed then and subsequently, and was proposed, at first, for the adoption and support of this Society and by its funds. This is the endowment of an agricultural professorship at the University of Virginia—or, it may be, more than one, if aided by other funds, and the liberality of the people of Virginia.

Other and not less important measures would be, the cautious and limited beginning of Geological and Agricultural Surveys and reports thereupon, either for separate counties or for any other stated and limited spaces of territory. The importance of a geological survey will not be over-estimated; and the effect of a proper agricultural and statistical survey, similar in plan to the truly great work formerly conducted under the direction of the British Board of Agriculture, may be estimated from the influence of that work on the agriculture of England.

The carrying through in any specified time of a system so great and complete, for the whole territory of Virginia, could not be effected, nor even thought of as a result to be produced by our spare funds, and with all the available aid in prospect. Neither would it be necessary, nor desirable, for the whole operation to be in progress at once, or to be completed, generally, in any early time. Even if funds were now abundant for the purpose, the much larger portion of the State is not yet ready for the undertaking—and but a small portion of our people would yet appreciate the benefit, or be desirous, or even ready to profit fully by agricultural surveys and investigations. But certainly there are now some counties, or other localities, already enough advanced in agricultural improvement to be greatly benefited by these measures, and whose cultivators would so highly appreciate the benefits, as to be willing to pay half the necessary expense—and also by other aid and information to forward the labors of the examiners and reporters of agricultural resources, merits, deficiencies and errors, of the several districts. If, for example, this Society chose to offer $1000, by an appropriation, for this object, and as a beginning and working of the plan, the appropriation should be offered in separate sums of $250 to each of the first four localities, (of any stated limits) that would severally advance an equal amount, to employ and pay well-qualified persons to examine and report fully upon the several sections of territory. In this manner, by the Society's offering $250, as much more would be added thereto from private contributions—or in default thereof, no expense would be incurred. There could be no contest, or struggle, for different places to have preference of selection, and the first benefits of surveys, because the designation would be made in the order of time in which offers of equal pecuniary aid would be made to the Society. No county would be thus examined, and its agriculture reported upon, that did not care enough for the benefit to be willing to pay half the expense. And the reports made of even a few of the most improved counties, in detached parts of the State, by as many different competent examiners, would serve not only to benefit the several counties, as it would principally, but also as instruction for all other lands of similar characters, or having like facilities for improvement and good management. The early labors of this kind would serve to prepare for and facilitate any succeeding surveys. And if, by possibility, there should be either failure or disappointment, in the results, the system could be suspended, or abandoned, at the close of the first, or of any later years' operations, without leaving any incumbrance for the future on the funds, or any obstacle to subsequently better devised plans and efforts of the Society, for its great object, the improvement of agriculture throughout the territory of Virginia.

At the meeting of the Farmers Assembly in 1856, the Executive Committee was required "to cause to be made a marble bust and a portrait of Philip St. George Cocke, Esq., to be bestowed as this body shall hereafter determine." The Executive Committee appointed William Boulware, Wm. H. Macfarland and R. H. Dulany, Esqrs., a committee to consult with Col. Cocke, and make necessary arrangements for having his bust and portrait made, in accordance with those instructions. The portrait has been completed by a distinguished artist, and is now in the possession of the Secretary of the Society, subject to the order of your body; and the causes which delayed the action of the Committee in the further execution of those instructions are set forth in their report, marked (D.)

The Committee take great pleasure in acknowledging the receipt, through the Hon. Wm. Ballard Preston, of Montgomery, of sixty-one valuable works on French Agriculture, which have been kindly tendered to the Society by M. Monny de Mornay, Director of the Department of Agriculture in France; and they have instructed their President to acknowledge, in suitable terms, their high appreciation of the valuable gift, and of the liberal spirit which prompted the gift. (See document E.)

By the Constitution of the Society, it is made the duty of the Executive Committee to arrange all the counties, cities and towns of Virginia, in which there are known resident Members of the Society into Electoral Districts, for the Election of Members of the Farmers' Assembly. By the recent arrangement there are sixty-nine Electoral Districts and one hundred and twenty-eight Members of the Farmers' Assembly.

The Treasurer's report and accounts (marked F) will be herewith submitted; also the entire journal of proceedings of the Executive Committee for the past year and for the preceding years.

By order of the Executive Committee.

EDMUND RUFFIN,
President of the Virginia State
Agricultural Society.

———

(A)

Expenses and Receipts of Annual Fairs since 1853.
EXPENSES—1853.

Incidental expenses, including advertising, Forage, &c............ $2.145 97

RECEIPTS.

Donation Madame Sontag...$ 100 00 ,
Gate Fees................... 1.947 17
                           ——————
                            $2.047 17

The police department paid by the city, a large part of the service being gratuitous.

EXPENSES—1854.

Incidental expenses	$1,311	32
Printing and advertising	215	62
Forage department	1,297	97
Police department	2,591	20
	$5,416	**11**

RECEIPTS.

Gate Fees	$3,289	50
Rents	200	00
Badges	707	30
City of Rich'd for police	1,000	00
	$5,196	**80**

—

EXPENSES—1855.

Office expenses		$ 338	78
Incidental	1,606 59		
Off expense of plate, &c.	535 00	1,071	59
Printing and advertising		263	50
Ticket office		130	75
Police department		2,807	24
Forage department		1,241	33
Repairs to Fair Grounds		593	54
		$6,446	**73**

RECEIPTS.

Gate Fees	$2,505	76
Badges	551	32
Rent	400	00
	$3,457	**08**

—

EXPENSES—1856.

Office expenses	$ 396	78
Printing and advertising, of which 447 for Farmers' Assembly	694	74
Incidental expenses	1,065	58
Ticket office	116	12
Police department	2,658	75
Forage department	958	97
Repairs to Fair Grounds	949	11
Rent of horse lot	500	00
	$7,340	**05**

RECEIPTS.

Gate Fees	$2,370	31
Badges	365	44
Rents	250	00
J. P. Ballard's donation on account of horse lot	166	67
	$3,152	**42**

—

EXPENSES—1857.

Office expenses	$ 96	67
Incidental expenses	654	76
Ticket office	86	00
Police department	1,849	50
Forage department	968	95
Repairs to Fair Grounds	630	90
Rent of horse lot	1,000	00
	$5,286	**78**

RECEIPTS.

Rents	$ 445	00
Gate Fees	2,843	62
City of Richmond for horse lot	1,000	00
	$4,288	**62**

The above statement shows the incidental receipts from the holding of the Fairs, and the incidental expenses attending them, except the premiums.

—

(B)

Refers to proceedings of the Executive Committee on the 27th November, 1857—the 27th of January following, and on the 27th of April, 1858, all which were contained in a card published by the Secretary in the October number of the Southern Planter, page 593.

—

(C)

At a meeting of the Executive Committee of the Virginia State Agricultural Society on the 26th of November, 1858, the following report was submitted by Mr. Knight and unanimously adopted:

The committee appointed to visit the Belona Arsenal property " to ascertain its condition, cost, the expense of establishing an Agricultural School thereat, and the expediency of accepting the property with that view" report: That they have visited the place, and made a full examination of the buildings, and found them to be in a very dilapidated condition, and in view of their condition and their arrangement, consider them unfit for the purposes of a school. They have not deemed it necessary to make an accurate estimate of the cost of repairs of the buildings, and of such alterations as would be needful to adapt them to the accommodation of a school, because it is very apparent that it would require an amount far beyond the present means of the Society. The committee, therefore, respectfully report against the expediency of accepting the property on the terms on which it has been tendered to the Society.

—

(D)

The committee appointed to have a portrait, and also a bust, prepared of the late President of the Society, Col. COCKE, report: That they contracted with Maurince Guillaume, a distinguished artist, for the portrait, and that it has been executed, and is now in the possession of the Secretary of the Society, at the Society's rooms, in the city of Richmond. They report further, that nothing has been done in reference to the bust, because it is believed it cannot be well executed in this country. * * *

WM. BOULWARE.

October 29, 1858.

—

(E)

SMITHFIELD, 26th Oct., 1858.

To the President of the
Agricultural Society of Va.:

SIR:—During a visit last year to Paris, I had the gratification of forming an acquaintance with the Honorable de Monny de Mornay, Director of the department of Agriculture for France.

Ardently devoted to agriculture as an elevated science and ennobling art, its chief direction in that great empire is entrusted to his care. His administration is characterized by wise and salutary measures for its improvement within his own country, as well as a comprehensive and liberal spirit, that anxiously seeks to diffuse the •benefits and blessings that science, knowledge and skill are constantly contributing toward its promotion.

In this spirit, and as a testimonial of the kind consideration and regard in which he holds our venerable Commonwealth, he requests me to present for him to the Agricultural Society of Virginia, a collection of works on agriculture, from the department over which he presides.

In his name I now present them to the Society, and in his behalf pray you will accept them. The collection consists of sixty-one volumes and pamphlets, accompanied by memoirs, beautiful and elegant engravings, illustrative of the various subjects treated of in the volumes, together forming a good collection of the best works on agriculture and horticulture recently published in France.

A catalogue is also furnished prepared by Mr. Alexander Vattemere, always active and distinguished in whatever contributes to the intellectual union or harmony of nations.

With high consideration and respect,
I am your ob'nt ser't,

WM. BALLARD PRESTON.

(F)

THE TREASURER'S ACCOUNT.

VIRGINIA STATE AGRICULTURAL SOCIETY,
In account with Ch. B. WILLIAMS, Treasurer.

Receipts within the year.

Donation of J. P. Ballard for rent (in part) of horse lot for 1856,	166 67
Donation from City of Richmond ditto for 1857,	1.000 00
Withdrawn from City Savings Bank,	1.400 00
Bills collected for forage department,	28 51
Interest account,	2.836 50
Permanent Fund Col. Townes 4th installment of his donation,	100 00
Permanent Fund for one life membership,	20 00
Contingent Fund, annual memberships,	3.913 26
Contingent Fund, paid by W. C. Rives, Esq., premium offered by him,	15 00
Contingent Fund, received for auction fees,	3 50
Contingent Fund, rent of booths,	445 00
Contingent Fund, gate money and premium,	2.843 62
Contingent Fund, sale of transactions,	4 00
Balance on hand per last settlement,	1·072 74
	$14.748 80

Disbursements within the year.

On account of premiums of 1854,	15 00	
Premiums of 1856,	37 00	
Premiums of 1857,	3.896 50	
Expenses of 1856–7,	94	
Rent of horse lot 1856,	216 51	
Rent of horse lot 1857,	976 49	
Salary of Secretary,	1.500 00	
Office expenses,	408 92	
Printing and advertising,	1.242 42	
Incidental expenses,	654 76	
Ticket office,	86 00	
Police Department,	1.849 50	
Forage Department,	997 46	
Repairs of Fair Grounds,	632 90	
Returned to Members twice p'd $3, counterfeit $5,	8 00	
Discount on uncur't fds.	4 48	
Deposit'd with City Savings Bank,	1.000 00	13.526 88
Balance,		$1.221 92

List of balances on 30th September, 1858.

Contingent Fund,		48.089 02
Permanent Fund,		46.364 00
Rent of horse lot 1857 (unclaimed,)		23 51
Interest account,		9.907 20
Cash,	1.221 92	
Virginia State stock,	500 00	
Richmond City stock,	44.750 00	
Am't carried forward,	$16.471 92	$104.383 73

Am't brought forward,	$46.471 92	$104.383 73
Premiums of 1853,	. 3.353 00	
Premiums of 1854,	. 3.843 50	
Premiums of 1855,	. 3.731 00	
Premiums of 1856,	. 3.805 60	
Premiums of 1857,	. 3.896 50	
Expenses of 1853–4,	. 3.884 24	
Expenses of 1854–5,	. 7.456 77	
Expenses of 1855–6,	. 8.958 44	
Expenses of 1856-7,	. 8.877 34	
Expenses of 1857–8,	. 7.343 45	
Rent of horse lot 1856,	162 57	
City Savings Bank,	. 2.600 00	
	$104.383 73	$104.383 73

GENERAL MEETING OF THE SOCIETY.

After the final adjournment of the meeting of the members elect of the Farmers Assembly on Wednesday the 3d of November, the members of the State Agricultural Society organized themselves into a general meeting for the discussion of subjects relating to the state and prospects of the Society. John R. Edmunds, Esq., was called to the chair.

On motion of Mr. W. C. Knight, of Nottoway,

Resolved, That a Committee be appointed to wait upon the Union Society, now in Session, and invite them to unite in the proceedings of this meeting. Committee—Messrs. Knight, Newton, and Garnett, of Henrico.

On motion of Mr. Seddon, after various propositions of amendment, and a free discussion, in which the members of both Societies participated, the following resolution was adopted with but two or three dissenting voices :

Resolved, That it be recommended to the Executive Committee of the State Agricultural Society to confer with the Executive Committee of the Union Agricultural Society on the practicability of a permanent union of the two Societies, and if found practicable, to report the terms of such union to the next meeting of the State Agricultural Society, or to the next Farmers' Assembly, as they may deem judicious.

The meeting then adjourned.

—

THURSDAY NIGHT, Nov. 4th, 1858.

The members of the Union Agricultural Society of Virginia and North Carolina, and of the Virginia State Agricultural Society, convened in joint meeting at the Market Street Baptist Church, at half-past seven o'clock, to hear the Annual Address.

The President introduced Professor Holcombe, of the University of Virginia, who had been invited by the Executive Committee to address the meeting on an interesting branch of the general subject of slavery :—
" The right of the State to institute Slavery, considered as a question of Natural Law, with special reference to African Slavery as it exists in the United States."

Professor Holcombe then delivered the following discourse :

Mr. President, and

　Gentlemen of the Agricultural Society :

It seems to me eminently proper, to connect with these imposing exhibitions of the trophies of your agricultural skill, a discussion of the whole bearings and relations, jural, moral, social, and economical, of that peculiar industrial system to which we are so largely indebted for the results that have awakened our pride and gratification. No class in the community has so many and such large interests gathered up in the safety and permanence of that system as the Farmers of the State. The mainwheel and spring of your material prosperity, interwoven with the entire texture of your social life, underlying the very foundations of the public strength and renown, to lay upon it any rash hand would put in peril whatever you value; the security of your property, the peace of your society, the well-being—if not the existence of that dependent race which Providence has committed to your guardianship—the stability of your government, the preservation in your midst of union, liberty, and civilization. By the introduction of elements of such inexpressible magnitude, the politics of our country have been invested with the grandeur and significance which belong to those great struggles upon which depend the destinies of nations. The mad outbreaks of popular passion, the rapid spread of anarchical opinions, the mournful decay of ancient patriotism, the wide disruption of Christian unity, which have marked the progress, and disclosed the power, purpose and spirit of this agitation, come home to your business and bosoms with impressive emphasis of warning and instruction. No pause in a strife around which cluster all the hopes and fears of freemen, can give any earnest of enduring peace, until the principles of law and order which cover with sustaining sanction all the relations of our society, have obtained their rightful ascendency over the reason and conscience of the Christian world.

The most instructive chapters in history are those of opinions. The decisive battle-fields of the world furnish but vulgar and deceptive indices of human progress. Its true eras are marked by transitions of sentiment and opinion. Those invisible moral forces that emanate from the minds of the great thinkers of the race, rule the courses of history. The recent awakening of our Southern mind upon the question of African Slavery, has been followed by a victory of peace, which, we trust, will embrace within its beneficent influence generations and empires yet unborn. Such was the strength of anti-slavery feeling within our own borders, that scarcely a quarter of a century has elapsed since an Act of Emancipation was almost consummated, under the auspices of our most intelligent and patriotic citizens; a measure which probably all would now admit bore in its womb elements of private distress and public calamity, that must have impressed upon our history, through ages of expanding desolation, the lines of fire and blood. But

"Whirlwinds fitliest scatter pestilence."

Nothing less than an extremity of peril could have induced a general revision of long-standing opinions, intrenched in formidable prejudices, and sanctioned by the most venerable authority. Slavery was explored, for the first time, with the forward and reverted eye of true statesmanship, under all the lights of history—of social and political philosophy—of natural and Divine law. Public sentiment rapidly changed its face. Every year of controversy has encouraged the advocates of "discountenanced truth" by the fresh accessions it has brought to their numbers, whilst no desertions have thinned the enlarging ranks. The celebrated declaration of Mr. Jefferson, that he knew no attribute of the Almighty which would take the side of the master in a contest with his slave, is so far from commanding the assent of the intelligent slaveholders of this generation, that the justice, the humanity, and the policy of the relation as it exists with us, has become the prevailing conviction of our people. Public honours, and gratitude, are the fitting meed of the statesmen, whether living or dead, (and amongst them I recall no names more eminent than those associated with the proudest traditions of this hospitable and patriotic city, Leigh, Gholson, and Brown,) who threw themselves into this imminent and deadly breach, and grappling with an uninformed and unreflecting sentiment, delivered the commonwealth, when in the very jaws of death, from moral, social and political ruin. Permit me to premise some words of explanation as to the meaning and extent of the subject upon which I have been invited to address this meeting. It presents no question of municipal or international law. It raises no inquiry as to the rightfulness of the means by which slavery was introduced into this continent, nor into the nature of the legal sanctions under which it now exists. There can be no doubt that slavery, for more than a century after it was established in the English colonies, was in entire harmony with the Common Law, as it was expounded by the highest judicial authorities, and with the principles of the Law of Nations, and of Natural Law as laid down in the writings of the most eminent publicists. At the commencement of our Revolution men were living who remembered the Treaty of Utrecht, by which, in the language of Lord Brougham, all the glories of Ramillies and Blenheim were bartered for a larger share in the lucrative commerce of the slave trade. But whatever may be our present opinions upon these subjects, the black race now constitutes an integral part of our community, as much so as the white, and the authority of the State to adjust their mutual relations can in no manner depend upon the method by which either was brought within its jurisdiction. The State in every age must provide a constitution and laws, if it does not find them in existence, adapted to its special wants and circumstances. African Slavery in the United States is consistent with Natural Law, because if all the bonds of public authority were suddenly dissolved, and the community called upon to reconstruct its social and political system, the relations of the two races remaining in other respects unaltered, it would be our right and duty to reduce the negro to subjection. To the phrase Natural Law, I shall attach in this discussion the signification in which it is generally used, and consider it as synonymous with justice; not that imperfect justice which may be discerned by the savage mind, but those ethical rules, or principles of right, which, upon the grounds of their own fitness and propriety, and irrespective of the sanction of Divine authority, commend themselves to the most cultivated human reason. Slavery we may define, so as to embrace all the elements that properly belong to it, as a condition or relation in which one man is charged with the protection and support of another, and invested with an absolute property in his labour, and such a degree of authority over his person as may be requisite to enforce its enjoyment. It is a form of involuntary restraint, extending to the personal as well as political liberty of the subject. The slave has sometimes, as at one period under the Roman jurisprudence, been reduced to a mere chattel, the power of the master over the person of the slave being as absolute as his property in his labour. This harsh and unnatural feature has never deformed the relation in any Christian country. In the United States the double character of the slave, as a moral person and as a subject of property, has been universally acknowledged, and to a greater or less degree protected, both by public sentiment and by the law of the land. It furnishes a key to the understanding of one of the most celebrated clauses in our Federal Constitution, as all know who are familiar with the luminous exposition, given by Mr. Madison in the Federalist, of its origin and meaning. In our own State, amongst other proofs of its recognition, we may point to the privilege conferred upon the master of emancipating his slave, and to the obligation imposed upon him of providing for his support when old, infirm, or insane; to the enactments which punish injuries to the slave, whether from a master or stranger, as offences of the same nature as if inflicted upon a white person, and to the construction placed by our courts upon the general language of criminal statutes, by which the slave, as a person, has been embraced within the range of their protection; to the regulations for the trial of slaves charged with the commission of crime, which, whilst they exact the responsibilities of moral agents, temper the administration of justice with mercy, and to the exemption from labour on the Lord's Day, an exemption which is shown by the provision for the Christian slave of a Jewish master, to have been established as a security for a right of

conscience. Indeed, he scarcely labours under any personal disability, to which we may not find a counterpart, in those which attach to those incompetent classes—the minor, the lunatic, and the married woman.

The statement of my subject presupposes the existence of the State. It thus assumes that there are involuntary restraints which may be rightfully imposed upon men, for the State itself is but the sum and expression of innumerable forms of restraint by which the life, liberty, and faculties of individuals are placed under the control of an authority independent of their volition? The truth that the selfishness of human nature, forces upon us the necessity of submitting to the discipline of law, or living in the license of anarchy, is too obvious to have required any argument in its support, in this presence. Until man becomes a law unto himself, society through a political organization must supply his want of self-control. Whether it may establish such a form of restraint, as personal slavery, cannot be determined until the principles upon which its authority should be exercised, have been settled, and the boundaries traced between private right and public power. The authority of the State must be commensurate with the objects for which it was established. Its function is, to reconcile the conflicting rights, and opposing interests, and jarring passions of individuals, so as to secure the general peace and progress. It proceeds upon the postulate, that society is our state of nature and that men by the primary law of their being, are bound to live and perfect themselves in fellowship with each other.

As God does not ordain contradictory and therefore impossible things, men can derive no rights from him which are inconsistent with the duration and perfection of society. The rights of the individual are not such as would belong to him, if he stood upon the earth like Campbell's imaginary "Last Man," amidst unbroken solitude, but such only as when balanced with the equal rights of other men, may be accorded to each, without injury to the rest. The necessities of social existence, then, not in the rudeness of the savage state, but under those complex and refined forms which have been developed by Christian civilization, constitute a horizon by which the unbounded liberty of nature is spanned and circumscribed.

This is no theory of social absolutism. It

does not make society the source of our rights, which therefore might be conferred or withheld at its caprice or discretion, but it does regard the just wants of society, as the measure and practical expression of their extent. It is no reproduction of the exploded error of the ancient statesmen, who inverting the natural relations of the parties, considered the aggrandizement of the State, without reference to the units of which it was composed, as the end of social union. The State was made for man, and not man for the State, but the coöperation of the State is yet so necessary to the perfection of his nature, that his interests require the renunciation of any claim inconsistent with its existence, or its value as an agency of civilization. It invades no province sacred to the individual, because the Divine Being who has rendered government a necessity, has made it a universal blessing, by ordaining a preestablished harmony between the welfare of the individual and the restraints which are requisite to the well-being of society.

Unless there is some fatal flaw in this reasoning, men have no rights which cannot be reconciled with the possession of a restraining power by the State, large enough to embrace every variety of injustice and oppression, for which society may furnish the occasion or the opportunity. The social union brings with it dangers and temptations, as well as blessings and pleasures— and men cannot fulfil the law and purpose of their being, unless the State has authority to protect the community from the tumultuous and outbreaking passions of its members, and to protect individuals as far as it can be accomplished without prejudice to the community, from the consequences of their own incompetence, improvidence and folly. Such are the natural differences between men in character and capacity, that without a steady and judicious effort by the State to redress the balance of privilege and opportunity which these inequalities constantly derange, the rich must grow richer, and the poor poorer, until even anarchy would be a relief to the masses, from the suffering and oppression of society. Owing likewise to this variety of condition, and of moral and intellectual endowment, it is impossible to prescribe any stereotype forms admitting of universal application, under which the restraining discipline of law should be exercised. The ends of social union remain the same through all ages, but the means of realizing those ends must be adapted to successive stages of advancement, and change with the varying intelligence and virtue of individuals, and classes, and races, and the local circumstances of different countries. The object being supreme in importance must carry with it as an incident, the right to employ the means which may be requisite to its attainment. The individual must yield property, liberty, life itself when necessary to preserve the life, as it were, of the collective humanity. To these principles, every enlightened government in the world, conforms its practice, protecting men not only from each other, but from themselves, graduating its restraints according to the character of the subject, and multiplying them with the increase of society in wealth, population and refinement. We cannot look into English or American jurisprudence without discovering innumerable forms of restraint upon rights of persons as well as rights of property, as in that absolute subordination of all personal rights to the general welfare, which lies at the foundation of the law for the public defence, the law to punish crimes, and the law to suppress vagrancy ; or in those qualified restraints by which the administration of justice between individuals, has been sometimes enforced, as in imprisonment for debt; or in that partial and temporary subjection of one person to the control of another, either for the benefit of the former, or upon grounds of public policy, presented in the law of parent and child, guardian and ward, master and apprentice, lunatic and committee, husband and wife, officer and soldiers of the army, captain and mariners of the ship. Whether we proceed in search of a general principle, which may ascertain the extent of the public authority by a course of inductive reasoning, or by an observation of the practice of civilized communities, we reach the same conclusions. The State must possess the power of imposing any restraint without regard to its form, which can be shown by an enlarged view of social expediency, or upon an indulgent consideration for human infirmity, to be beneficial to its subject, or necessary to the general well-being.

In the legislation of Congress for the Indian tribes within our territory, and in that of great Britain for the alien and dependent nations under her jurisdiction, we see how the public authority, as flexible as comprehensive in its grasp, accommodates itself to the weakness and infirmity of races, as well as of individuals. Upon what principles is the British government administered in the East? In 1833, on the application of the East India Company for a renewal of its charter, they were explained and defended by Macaulay in a speech which would have delighted Burke, as much by its practical wisdom, as its glittering rhetoric. An immense society was placed under the almost despotic rule of a few strangers. No securities were provided for liberty or property, which an Englishman would have valued. This system of servitude was vindicated, not on the grounds of abstract propriety, but of its adaptation to the wants and circumstances of those upon whom it was imposed. India, it was urged, constituted a vast exception to all those general rules of political science which might be deduced from the experience of Europe. Her population was disqualified by character and habit, for the rights and privileges of British freemen. In their moral and social amelioration, under British rule, was to be found the best proof of its justice and policy. It was a despotism no doubt, but it was a mild and paternal one; and no form of restraint less stringent could be substituted with equal advantage to those upon whom it was to operate. It has often occurred to me in reading those fervid declamations upon Southern slavery, with which this great orator has inflamed the sensibilities of the British public, that his lessons of sober and practical statesmanship, from which no English ministry has ever departed, might be turned with irresistible recoil upon their author. Was American slavery introduced by wrong and violence? India was "stripped of her plumed and jewelled turban," by rapine and injustice. Are the relations of England to India, so anomalous that it would be unsafe to accept generalizations drawn from the experience of other communities? History might be interrogated in vain, for a parallel to the condition of our Southern society. Are the Hindoos unfit for liberty? Not more so than the African. Is despotism necessary in India, because it is problematical whether crime could be repressed or social order preserved under more liberal institutions? The danger of license and anarchy would be far more imminent, from an emancipation of our slaves. If the statesman despairs of making brick without straw in the East, can he expect to find the problem easier in the West? Has the Hindoo improved in arts and morals under the beneficent sway of his British master? In the transformation of the African savage into the Christian slave, the relative advance has been immeasurably greater. The truth is, that the principles which lie at the foundation of all political restraint, may make it the duty of the State under certain circumstances, to establish the relation of personal servitude. All forms of restraint involve the exercise of power over the individual without his consent. All are inconsistent with any theory of natural right which claims for man, a larger measure of liberty than can be reconciled with the peace and progress of the society in which he lives. All operate harshly at times upon individuals. All are reflections upon human nature, are alike wrong in the abstract. Any is right in the concrete, when necessary to the welfare of the community in which it exists, or beneficial to the subject upon whom it is imposed. If society may establish the institution of private property, involving restrictions by which the majority of mankind are shut out from all access to that great domain which the author of nature has stocked with the means of subsistence for his children, and justify a restraint so comprehensive and onerous, by its tendency to promote civilization; if it may discriminate between classes and individuals, and apportion to some a larger measure of political liberty than it does to others; if it may take away life, liberty or property when demanded by the public good: if, as in various personal relations, it may protect the helpless and incompetent, by placing them under a guardianship proportioned in the term and extent of its authority to the degree and duration of the infirmity; why if a commensurate necessity arises, and the same great ends are to be accomplished, is its claim to impose upon an inferior race the degree of personal restraint which may be requisite to coerce and direct its labour, to be treated as a usurpation? The authority of the State under proper circumstances, to establish a system of slavery, is one question; the existence of those circumstances, or the expediency of such legislation is another and entirely distinct question. No doubt a much smaller capacity for self-control, and a much lower degree of intelligence must concur, to justify personal slavery, than would be sufficient to impart validity to other forms of subordination. No doubt the public authority upon this as upon every other subject, may be abused by the selfish passions and interests of men. But once acknowledge the right of society to establish a government of pains and penalties, for the protection of the individual and the promotion of the general welfare, then unless it can be shown that slavery can in no instance be necessary to the well being of the community, or conducive to the happiness of the subject, (a proposition which is inconsistent with the admission of all respectable British and American abolitionists that any plan of emancipation in the Southern States, should be gradual and not immediate;) once make this fundamental concession, and the rightfulness of slavery, like that of every other form of restraint, becomes a question of time, place, men and circumstances.

The people of the United States accepting without much reflection, those expositions of human rights embodied in the infidel philosophy of France, and glowing with that generous enthusiasm to communicate the blessings of liberty which is always inspired by its possession, have been disposed to look with common aversion upon all forms of unequal restraint. Ravished by the divine airs of their own freedom, they have imagined that its strains, like those heard by the spirit in Comus, might create a soul under the ribs of death. Forgetting the ages through whose long night their fathers wrestled for this blessing, they have regarded an equal liberty, as the universal birthright of humanity. Hence, as they have witnessed nation after nation throwing off its old political bondage, and in the first transports of emotion, "shedding the grateful tears of new-born freedom" over the broken chains of servitude, they have welcomed them into the glorious fellowship of republican States, with plaudit, and sympathy, and benediction. But, alas! the crimes which have been committed in the name of liberty, the social disorder and political convulsion which have attended its progress, if they have not broken the power of its spells over the heart, have dispersed the illusions of our understanding. What has become of France, Italy, Greece, Mexico, Spanish America? that stately fleet of freedom, which when first launched upon the seas of time, with all its bravery on, was "courted by every wind that held it play." A part has been swallowed up in the gulfs of anar-chy and despotism—the rest still float above the wave, but with rudder and anchor gone, stripped of every bellying sail and steadying spar, they only serve,

"Like ocean wrecks, to illuminate the storm."

The melancholy experience of both hemispheres has compelled all but the projectors of revolution to acknowledge, that the forms of liberty are valueless without its spirit, and that an attempt to outstrip the march of Providence, by conferring it on a people unprepared for its enjoyments by habit, tradition, or character, is an indescribable folly—which instead of establishing peace, order and justice, will be more likely to inaugurate a reign of terror and crime in which civilization itself may perish.

If the justice or fitness of slavery is to be determined, like other forms of involuntary restraint, not by speculative abstractions, but by reference to its adaptation to the wants and circumstances of the community in which it is established, and especially of the people over whom it is imposed, it only remains that we should apply these principles to the question of African Slavery in the United States. I shall not defend it as the only relation between the races, in which the superior can preserve the civilization that renders life dear and valuable. This proposition can indeed be demonstrated by plenary evidence, and it is sufficient by itself to acquit the slaveholder of all guilt in the eye of morals. But if the system could be vindicated upon no higher ground, every generous spirit would grieve over the mournful necessity which rendered the degradation of the black man indispensable to the advancement of the white. Providence has condemned us to no such cruel and unhappy fate. The relation in our society is demanded by the highest and most enduring interests of the slave, as well as the master. It exists and must be preserved for the benefit of both parties. Duty is indeed the tenure of the master's right. Upon him there rests a moral obligation to make such provision for the comfort of the slave, as after proper consideration of the burthens and casualities of the service, can be deemed a fair compensation for his labour; to allow every innocent gratification compatible with the steady, though mild discipline, as necessary to the happiness as the value of the slave; to furnish the means and facilities for religious instruction; and to contribute, as far and fast as a proper regard to the public safety will permit, to his general elevation and improvement. For oppression or injustice, allow me to say, I have no excuse to offer. I am willing to accept the sentiment of the heathen philosopher, and to regard a man's treatment of his slaves as a test of his virtue. And whenever a slaveholder is found who so far forgets the sentiments of humanity, the feelings of the gentleman, and the principles of the Christian, as to abuse the authority which the law gives him over his slaves, I trust that a righteous and avenging public sentiment will pursue him with the scorn and degradation which attend the husband or father, who by cruel usage makes home intolerable to wife or child.

Personal and political liberty are both requisite to develop the highest style of man. They furnish the amplest opportunities for the exercise of that self-control which is the germ and essence of every virtue, and for that expansive and ameliorating culture by which our whole nature is exalted in the scale of being, and clothed with the grace, dignity and authority, becoming the lords of creation. Whenever the population of a State is homogeneous, although slavery may perform some important functions in quickening the otherwise tardy processes of civilization, it ought to be regarded as a temporary and provisional relation. If there are no radical differences of physical organization or moral character, the barriers between classes are not insurmountable. The discipline of education and liberal institutions, may raise the serf to the level of the baron.— Against any artificial circumscription seeking to arrest that tendency to freedom which is the normal state of every society of equals, human nature would constantly rise in rebellion. But where two distinct races are collected upon the same territory, incapable from any cause of fusion or severance, the one being as much superior to the other in strength and intelligence as the man to the child, there the rightful relation between them is that of authority upon the one side, and subordination in some form, upon the other. Equality, personal and political, could not be established without inflicting the climax of injustice upon the superior, and of cruelty on the inferior race: for if it were possible to preserve such an arrangement, it would wrest the sceptre of dominion from the wisdom and strength of society, and surrender it to its weakness and folly. "Of all

rights of man," says Carlyle, "the right of the ignorant man to be guided by the wiser, to be gently and firmly held in the true course, is the indispensablest. Nature has ordained it from the first. Society struggles towards perfection by conforming to and accomplishing it, more and more. If freedom have any meaning, it means enjoyment of this right, in which all other rights are enjoyed. It is a divine right and duty on both sides, and the sum of all social duties between the two." Under the circumstances I have supposed, no intelligent man could hesitate, except as to the form of subordination: nor has entire equality been ever allowed in society where the inferior race constituted an element of any magnitude.

Personal servitude is generally the harshest and most objectionable form of restraint, exposing its subjects to an abuse of power involving greater suffering than any other. But this is not an invariable law, even in a homogeneous society. The most recent researches into the condition of the labouring classes of Europe, the descendants of the emancipated serfs, have satisfied all candid inquirers after truth that a large number have sunk below the level of their ancient slavery, and would be thankful to belong to any master who would furnish them with food, clothing and shelter. But when we are settling the law of a society embracing in its bosom distinct and unequal races, the problem is complicated by elements which create the gravest doubt whether personal liberty will prove a blessing or a curse. It may become a question between the slavery, and the extinction or further deterioration of the inferior race. Thus, if it is difficult to procure the means of subsistence from density of population or other cause, and if the inferior race is incapable of sustaining a competition with the superior in the industrial pursuits of life, a condition of freedom which would involve such competition, must either terminate in its destruction, or consign it to hopeless degradation. If, under these circumstances, a system of personal servitude gave reasonable assurance of preserving the inferior race, and gradually imparting to it the amelioration of a higher civilization, no Christian statesman could mistake the path of duty. Natural law, illuminated in its decision by History, Philosophy, and Religion, would not only clothe the relation with the sanction of justice, but lend to it the lustre of mercy. It will not, I apprehend, be difficult to show that all these conditions apply to African slavery in the United States. Look at the races which have been brought face to face in unmanageable masses, upon this continent, and it is impossible to mistake their relative position. The one still filling that humble and subordinate place, which as the pictured monuments of Egypt attest, it has occupied since the dawn of history; a race which during the long-revolving cycles of intervening time has founded no empire, built no towered city, invented no art, discovered no truth, bequeathed no everlasting possession to the future, through law-giver, hero, bard, or benefactor of mankind: a race which, though lifted immeasurably above its native barbarism by the refining influence of Christian servitude has yet given no signs of living and self-sustaining culture. The other, a great composite race which has incorporated into its bosom all the vital elements of human progress; which, crowned with the traditions of history and bearing in its hands the most precious trophies of civilization, still rejoices in the overflowing energy, the abounding strength, the unconquerable will which have made it "the heir of all the ages;" and which with aspirations unsatisfied by centuries of toil and achievement, still vexes sea and land with its busy industry, binds coy nature faster in its chains, embellishes life more prodigally with its arts, kindles a wider inspiration from the fountain lights of freedom, follows knowledge,

> "like a sinking star,
> Beyond the utmost bound of human thought,"

and pushing its unresting columns still further into the regions of eldest Night, in lands more remote than any over which Roman eagles ever flew, "to the farthest verge of the green earth," plants the conquering banner of the Cross,

> "Encircling continents and oceans vast,
> In one humanity."

It is impossible to believe that the supremacy in which the Caucasian has towered over the African through all the past can be shaken, or that the black man can ever successfully dispute the preeminence with his white brother as members of the same community, in the arts and business of life. Could such races be mated with each other? It is unnecessary to refer to Egypt or Central America, where a mongrel population, *monumenta veneris nefandæ*, exhibit the de-

teriorating influence of a similar fusion. If there were no broad and indelible dividing lines of colour and physical organization to keep the black and white races apart, their respective traditions, extremes of moral and intellectual advancement, and unequal aptitudes, if not capacities for higher civilization, separate them by an impassible gulf. That feeble remnant of our kindred, who, surrounded by hordes of barbarians, yet linger among the deserted seats of West India civilization, may forget the dignity of Anglo-Saxon manhood, in the despair and poverty to which they have been reduced by British injustice; but we "sprung of earth's first blood," and "foremost in the files of time," who under Providence are masters of our destiny, will never permit the generations of American history to be bound together by links of shame. Is the deportation of the African race practicable? A more extravagant project was never seriously entertained by the human understanding. There are economical considerations alone, which would render it utterly hopeless. The removal of our black population would create a gap in the industry of the world, which no white immigration could fill. It would bring over the general prosperity of the country a blight and ruin, that would dry up all the sources of revenue on which the success of the measure would depend. Its consequences would not terminate with this continent. The great wheel which moves the commerce and manufactures of the world, would be arrested in its revolutions. General bankruptcy would follow a shock, besides which the accumulated financial crises of centuries would be unfelt. In the recklessness and despair of crime and famine thus induced, the ancient landmarks of empire might be disturbed, and all existing governments shaken to their foundation. No favorable inference can be drawn from immense emigration, which, like the swell of a mighty sea, is pouring upon our shores. It comes from regions where population is too dense for subsistence and where a vacant space is closed as soon as it is opened. It is impelled by double influences, neither of which can operate to any extent upon the American slave, want and wretchedness at home, and all material and moral attractions abroad. It is composed of men accustomed at least to personal freedom, and belonging to races endowed with far more energy and intelligence than the African. It is received into a community, whose strength and vitality enable it to absorb and assimilate a much larger foreign element than any of which history has any record. If the black man was able and willing to return to his native land, he must carry with him the habits and feelings of the slave. Can it be supposed that such a living cloud as the annual increase of our slaves, could discharge its contents into the bosom of any African society, without blighting in the license of their first emancipation from all restraint, whatever promise of civilization it might have held out.

If we must accept the permanent residence of this race upon our soil, as a providential arrangement beyond human control, it only remains to adjust the form of its subordination. Should it embrace personal, as well as political servitude? Personal slavery surrounds the black man with a protection and salutary control which his own reason and energies are incapable of supplying, and by converting elements of destruction into sources of progress, promotes his physical comfort, his intellectual culture, and his moral amelioration. Emancipation upon the other hand in any form, gradual or immediate, would either destroy the race through a wasting process of poverty, vice, and crime, or sink it into an irrecoverable deep of savage degradation. What Homer has said may be true, that a free man loses half his value the day he becomes a slave; but it is quite as true, that the slave who is converted into a freeman, is more likely to lose the remaining half than to recover what is gone. There are no rational grounds upon which we could anticipate for our slaves, an advancing civilization if they were emancipated, or upon which we could expect them to preserve their contented temper, their material comfort, their industrious habits, and their general morality. The negro has learned much in contact with the white man, but he is yet ignorant of that great art which is the guardian of all acquisition, the art of self-goverment. The superiority of the white man in skill, energy, foresight, providence, aptitude for improvement, and control over the lower appetites and passions, would give him a decisive and fatal advantage in the pitiless competition of life. The light which history sheds around this problem, is broad and unchanging. Wherever unequal races are brought together, unless reduced by despotism to an indiscriminate servitude, or mingled by a deteriorating and demoralizing fusion, the inferior must choose between slavery and extinction. Upon these principles only can we explain the preservation of the Indian inhabitants of Spanish America, and the destruction of the aboriginal races which have crossed the path of English colonization. All the lower stages of civilization are characterized by an improvidence of the future and a predominance of the animal nature, which increase the force of temptation, and at the same time diminish the power of resistance. Hence it is, that when an inferior race, animated by the passions of the savage, but destitute of the restraining self-control which is developed by civilization, is brought in contact with a higher form of social existence, where the stimulants and facilities for sensual gratification are multiplied, and the consequences of excess and improvidence aggravated in fatality, it is mown down by a mortality more terrific than the widest waste of war. Private charity and the influence of Christianity upon individuals may retard the operation of these causes, but destruction is only a question of time. Without a judicious husbandry of the surplus proceeds of labour in the day of prosperity to meet the demands of age, sickness and casualty, poverty alone with the disease, suffering and crime that attend it, would wear out any labouring population. The remnant of the Indian tribes scattered along the lower banks of the St. Lawrence, present an impressive illustration of these simple political truths. "They manifest," says Prof. Bowen, "sufficient industry when the reward of labour is immediate: but surrounded by an abundance of fertile and cleared land, where others would grow rich, they are rapidly perishing from improvidence alone."

Even in England, in periods of manufacturing prosperity, when wages are high, the Chancellor of the Exchequer reckons with as much confidence upon the expenditure by the operatives of their surplus profits, in spirits, tobacco, and other hurtful stimulants, as upon the proceeds of the income tax.— And if the working class of England, instead of being constantly recruited from a higher order of society, consisted of an inferior race, the annual losses from intemperance and improvidence would soon carry it off. As population becomes denser, our free blacks are destined to exemplify the same great law. In the free States, where an encroaching tide of white emigration is driving them from one field of industry after another, they already stand, as the statistics of population, disease and crime disclose, upon the narrowest isthmus which can divide life from death. When we remember that the destructive agencies which would be let loose amongst our slaves, by emancipation, are as fatal to morals as to life, and that the natural inequality between the races would be increased by a constant accession of numbers to the white through emigration, it is not extravagant to assert that exterminating massacre would involve a swifter, but scarcely more certain or more cruel death.

If emancipation took place in a tropical region, where climate forbade the competition of white labour, and the exuberance of nature supplied the means of life without the necessity of intelligent and systematic industry, there are other causes which would remove from the slave every safeguard of progress, and render his relapse into barbarism inevitable. Civilization depends upon activity, development, progress. It is measured by our wants and our work. Without indulging in any rash generalizations, we may safely affirm, that where animal life can be sustained without labour, and an enervating climate invites to indolent repose, we cannot expect from that class of society upon whom in every country the cultivation of the soil depends, any industrious emulation. So powerful is the influence of these physical causes over barbarous tribes, that under the torrid zone, as we are informed by Humboldt, where a beneficent hand has profusely scattered the seeds of abundance, indolent and improvident man experiences periodically a want of subsistence which is unfelt in the sterile regions of the North. As men increase in virtue and intelligence, they become more capable of resisting the operation of climate and other natural laws, but some form of slavery has been the only basis upon which civilization has yet rested in any tropical country. If it can be sustained upon any other, it must be by a race endowed with a larger fund of native energy than the African, or quickened by the electric power of a higher culture than he has ever possessed. His moral and physical conformation predispose him to indolence. *Cœlum non animum mutant,* has been the law of his history. Under the *Code Rural* of Hayti, the harshest compulsion has been used to subdue the sloth of barbarism, and

to compel the labour of the free black man, but in vain. In the British West Indies, since emancipation, no expedients have proven effectual to conquer this repugnance to exertion. The English historian, Alison, who, whatever may be his political sentiments, has no sympathies with slavery, in his last volume, thus describes the result of the experiment. " But disastrous as the results of the change have been to British interests both at home and in the West Indies, they are as nothing to those which have ensued to the negroes themselves, both in their native seats and the Trans-Atlantic Colonies. The fatal gift of premature emancipation has proved as pernicious to a race as it always does to an individual : the boy of seventeen sent out into the world, has continued a boy, and does as other boys do. The diminution of the agricultural exported produce of the islands to less than a half, proves how much their industry has declined. The reduction of their consumption of the British produce and manufactures in a similar proportion, tells unequivocally how much their means of comfort and enjoyment have fallen off. Generally speaking, the incipient civilization of the negro has been arrested by his emancipation : with the cessation of forced labour, the habits which spring from and compensate it, have disappeared, and savage habits and pleasures have resumed their ascendency over the sable race. The attempts to instruct and civilize them have, for the most part, proved a failure ; the *dolce far niente* equally dear to the unlettered savage as to the effeminate European, has resumed its sway ; and the emancipated Africans dispersed in the woods, or in cabins erected amidst the ruined plantations, are fast relapsing into the state in which their ancestors were when first torn from their native seats by the rapacity of a Christian avarice." A melancholy confirmation of this statement is furnished by a fact which I have learned from a reliable private source, that the prevailing crimes of this population have changed from petty larceny to felonies of the highest grades. But if the black race could escape barbarism, or defy those destroying elements of society, poverty and crime, there is a more comprehensive political induction which establishes the justice and expediency of its subjection to servitude. If in any community there is an inferior race which is condemned by permanent and irresistible causes to occupy the condition of a working class, not as independent proprietors of the soil they till, but as labourers for hire, then a system of personal slavery under which the welfare of the slave could be connected with the interest of the master, would be far preferable to the collective servitude of a degraded caste. This proposition supposes the existence, not of an inferior class simply, but an inferior race—which, as such, is condemned by nature to wear the livery of servitude in some form—which can never be quickened or sustained by those animating prospects of wealth, dignity and power which, in a homogeneous community, pour a renovating stream of moral health through every vein and artery of social life—which must earn a scanty and precarious subsistence by a stern, unintermitting and unequal struggle with selfish capital. Can any skepticism resist the conviction that, under such circumstances, a social adjustment which would engage the selfish passions of the superior race to provide for the comfort of the inferior, must be an arrangement of mercy as well as of justice? Upon this question the experience of England is full of instruction. The abolition of slavery upon the continent of Europe gradually converted the original serfs into owners of the soil. In England, it terminated with personal manumission—leaving the villein to work as a labourer for wages, or to farm as a tenant upon lease. What has been the effect of this great social revolution? I do not refer to that saturnalia of poverty, misery, vagrancy, and crime which immediately followed the disruption of the old feudal bonds, and the adjustment of the new relations of lord and vassal, by the "cold justice of the laws of political economy." What is the present condition of the English labourer? English writers, whose fidelity and accuracy are above suspicion, have almost exhausted the power of language in describing his abject wretchedness and squalid misery. They have distributed their population into the rich, the comfortable, the poor, and the perishing. That "bold peasantry, their country's pride," has almost disappeared. Every improvement in an industrial process which diminishes the amount of human labour, brings with it more or less of suffering to the English operative. Every scarce harvest, every fluctuation in trade, every financial crisis exposes him to beggary or starvation. In the selfish competition between the capitalist and

workman, says a distinguished christian philanthropist, " the capitalist, whether farmer, merchant, or manufacturer, plays the game, wins all the high stakes, takes the lion's share of the profits, and throws all the losses, involving pauperism and despair, upon the masses." Nothing can be more hopeless than the condition of the agricultural labourer. All the life of England, says Bowen in his lectures on Political Economy, " is in her commercial and manufacturing classes. Outside of the city walls, we are in the middle ages again. There are the nobles and the serfs, true castes, for nothing short of a miracle can elevate or depress one who is born a member of either." Moral and intellectual culture cannot be connected with physical destitution and suffering. We are not therefore surprised to learn, from a recent British Quarterly, that there is an overwhelming class of outcasts at the bottom of their society whom the present system of popular education does not reach, who are below the influence of religious ordinances, and scarcely operated upon by any wholesome restraint of public opinion. For the relief of this wretchedness an immense pauper system has grown up, as grinding in its exactions upon the rich, as demoralizing in its bounties to the poor. But even this frightful evil appears insignificant, in comparison with that embittered and widening feud between the classes of society, which has filled the most sanguine friends of human progress with the apprehension, that England's greatest danger may spring from the despair of her own children, the beggars who gaze in idleness and misery at her wealth, the savages who stand by the side of her civilization, and the heathen who have been nursed in the bosom of her Christianity. The intelligent philanthropists of England, place their whole hope of remedy in plans of colonization—plans for substituting coöperative associations for the system of hired service—plans for increasing the number of peasant proprietors, and thus placing labour on a more independent basis—for educating the working class, and for legislation which will facilitate the circulation of capital, and the more 'equal distribution of property. But if this evil working in the heart in the nation be incurable, if the helotism of the working classes should prove, as it has already been pronounced, irretrievable, I am far from advocating a reduction of the English labourer to slavery. There is no radical distinction of race, between the labourer and the capitalist. The latter owes his superiority, not to nature, but to the vantage ground of opportunity. Nature has implanted a consciousness of equality, so deeply in the bosom of the labourer, that personal slavery would bring with it a sense of degradation he could never endure. Whatever the general destitution and sufferings of his class, an undying hope will ever whisper to the individual that a happy fortune may raise him to comfortable independence, or social consideration. The very thought, that from his loins may spring some stately figure to tread, with dignity the shining eminences of life, is able to alleviate many hours of despondency. But above all, an instinctive love of liberty, such as was felt by the Spartan when he compared it to the sun, the most brilliant, and at the same time, the most useful object in creation, cherished in the Englishman by the traditions of centuries of struggle in its achievement and defence, cause him to echo the sentiment of his own poet,

"Bondage is winter, darkness, death, despair,
Freedom, the sun, the sea, the mountains and
    the air."

I fully subscribe to an opinion which has been expressed by an accomplished Southern writer, that an attempt to enslave the English labourer would equal, though it could not exceed in folly, an attempt to liberate the American slave—either seriously attempted and with sufficient power to oppose the natural current of events would overwhelm the civilization of the continent in which it occurred in anarchy. But if the English labourer belonged to a different race from his employer; if they were separated by a moral and intellectual disparity such as divides the Southern slave from his master : if instead of the sentiments and traditions of liberty which would make bondage worse than death, he had the gentle, tractable and submissive temper that adapt the African to servitude, who can doubt that a slavery which would insure comfort and kindness, would improve his condition in all its aspects?

None of the circumstances which prevent the application of the general proposition we have been discussing to the English labourer, extend to the American slave—none of the plans which have been suggested for the relief of the former would offer any hope of amelioration to the latter. No man who knows anything of the negro character, can for a moment suppose that the land of the country, could be distributed between them as tenant proprietors. If it was given to them to day, their improvidence would make it the property of the white man to morrow. Indeed the fact to which Mr. Webster called attention, that the products of the slave-holding States are destined mainly, not for the immediate consumption, but for purposes of manufacture and commercial exchange, exclude the possibility of an extended system of tenant proprietorship, and render cultivation and disposal by capital upon a large scale indispensable. The black man if emancipated must work for hire. Would he be better able to hold his own against the capitalist than the English labourer? Would not the misery and degradation of the latter, but faintly foreshadow the doom of the emancipated slave? His days embittered and shortened by privation; cheered by no hope of a brighter future; the burthens of liberty without its privileges; the degradation of bondage without its compensations; "the name of freedom graven on a heavier chain;" his root in the grave, the liberated negro under the influence of moral causes as irresistible as the laws of gravity, would moulder earthward. What is there, may I not ask, in the misery and desolation of this collective servitude, to compensate for the sympathy, kindness, comfort, and protection which so generally solace the suffering, and sweeten the toil, and make tranquil the slumber, and contented the spirits of the slave, whose lot has been cast in the sheltering bosom of a Southern home?

The approximation to equality in numbers, which has been hastily supposed to render emancipation safer than in the West Indies, would give rise to our greatest danger. It will not be long before the unmixed white population of the West Indies will be reduced, by the combined influences of emigration and amalgamation, to a few factors in the sea ports. In the United States, not only would the exodus of either race, or their fusion, be impracticable, but the pride of civilization, which now stoops with alacrity to bind up the wounds of the slave, would spurn the aspiring contact of the free man. The points of sympathy between master and slave may not be as numerous or powerful as we could desire, but between the white and the black man, in any society in which they are recognised as equals, and in which the latter are sufficiently numerous to create apprehension as to the consequences of distrust and aversion, a growing ill-will would deepen into irreconcilable animosity. Look at the isolation in which, notwithstanding their insignificance as a class, the free blacks of the North now live. "The negro," says De Tocqueville, "is free, but he can share neither the rights, nor the pleasures, nor the labour, nor the affections, nor the altar, nor the tomb of him whose equal he has been declared to be. He meets the white man upon fair terms, neither in life nor in death." What could be expected from a down-trodden race, existing in masses large enough to be formidable, in whose bosoms the law itself nourished a sense of injustice by proclaiming an equality which Nature and society alike denied, with passions unrestrained by any stake in the public peace, or any bonds of attachment to the superior class, but that it should seek in some frenzy of despair, to shake off its doom of misery and degradation? Would not the atrocities which have always distinguished a war of races, be perpetrated on a grander and more appalling scale than the world has ever yet witnessed? The recollections of hereditary feud alone have, in every age, so inflamed the angry passions of our nature as to lend a deeper gloom even to the horrors of war. When the poet describes the master of the lyre, as seeking to rouse the martial ardour of the Grecian conqueror and his attendant nobles, he brings before them the ghosts of their Grecian ancestors that were left unburied on the plains of Troy, who tossing their lighted torches—

"Point to the Persian abodes,
And glittering temples of their hostile gods."

But what would be the ferocity awakened in half-savage bosoms, when embittered memories of long-descended hate towards a superior race, exasperated by the maddening pangs of want, impelled them to seek retribution for centuries of imaginary wrong? Either that precious harvest of civilization which has been slowly ripening under the toils of successive generations of our fathers, and the genial sunshine and refreshing showers of centuries of kindly Providence, would be gathered by the rude sons of spoil, or peace would return after a tragedy of crime and sorrow, with whose burthen of woe the voice of history would be tremulous through long ages of after time.

The whole reasoning of modern philanthropy upon this subject has been vitiated, by its overlooking those fundamental moral differences between the races, which constitute a far more important element in the political arrangements of society, than relative intellectual power. It is immaterial how these differences have been created. Their existence is certain; and if capable of removal at all, they are yet likely to endure for such an indefinite period, that in the consideration of any practical problem, we must regard them as permanent. The collective superiority of a race can no more exempt it from the obligations of justice and mercy, than the personal superiority of an individual; but where unequal races are compelled to live together, a sober and intelligent estimate of their several aptitudes and capacities must form the basis of their social and political organization. The intellectual weakness of the black man is not so characteristic, as the moral qualities which distinguish him from his white brother. The warmest friends of emancipation, amongst others the late Dr. Channing, have acknowledged that the civilization of the African, must present a different type from that of the Caucasian, and resemble more the development of the East than the West. His nature is made up of the gentler elements. Docile, affectionate, light-hearted, facile to impression, reverential, he is disposed to look without for strength and direction. In the courage that rises with danger, in the energy that would prove a consuming fire to its possessor, if it found no object upon which to spend its strength, in the proud aspiring temper which would render slavery intolerable, he is far inferior to other races. Hence, subordination is as congenial to his moral, as a warm latitude is to his physical nature. Freedom is not "chartered on his manly brow" as on that of the native Indian. Unkindness awakens resentment, but servitude alone carries no sense of degradation fatal to self-respect. A civilization like our own could be developed only by a free people; but under a system of slavery to a superior race, which was ameliorated by the charities of our religion, the African is capable of making indefinite progress. He is not animated by that love of liberty which Bacon quaintly compared to a spark that ever flieth in the face of him who seeketh to trample it under foot. The masses of the old world, under various forms of slavery, have exhibited a standing discontent, and their struggles for freedom have been the flashes of a smothered but deeply hidden fire. The obedience of the African, unless disturbed by some impulse from without, and to which he yields only in a vague hope of obtaining respite from labour, is willing and cheerful. De Tocqueville, in his work on the French Revolution, points out a difference between nations, in what he calls the sublime taste for freedom—some seeking it for its material blessings only, others for its intrinsic attractions; and adds, "that he who seeks freedom for anything else than freedom's self, is made to be a slave." How fallacious must be any political induction which transfers to the African that love of personal liberty, which wells from the heart of our own race in a spring-tide of passionate devotion, the winters of despotism could never chill. The Providence which appointed the Anglo-Saxon to lead the van of human progress fitted him for his mission, by preconfiguring his soul to the influences of freedom. This sentiment is indestructible in his nature. It would survive the degradation of any form or term of bondage. Like the sea shell, when torn from its home in the deep, his heart, through all the ages of slavery, would be vocal with the music of his native liberty.

The strength of that security against oppression which the Southern slave derives from the selfishness of human nature, has never been sufficiently appreciated, for, in truth, it has existed in connection with no other form of servitude. With exceptions too slight to deserve remark, in Greece and Rome, in the British and Spanish colonies, it was cheaper to buy slaves than to raise them, to work them to death, than to provide for them in life. Hence in Rome, the slaves of the public were better cared for than those of the individual. With us, the master has a large and immediate interest, not only in the life, but the health, comfort and improvement of his slave, for they all add to his value and efficiency as a labourer. Southern slavery must therefore be tried upon its own merits, and not by data true or false, collected from other forms of servitude. Arithmetic, Gibbon once said, is the natural enemy of rhetoric, and a single statement will suffice to discredit all the reasoning, and pour contempt upon all the declamation which has confounded our slavery with that of the British West Indies. From the most re-

liable calculations that can be made, says Carey, in his Essay on the Slave Trade, it appears that for every African imported into the United States, ten are now to be found, such has been the wonderful growth of population; for every three imported into the British West Indies, only one now exists, such has been its frightful decline. But however ample this protection may be to the slave from the oppression of strangers, his own passions, it is urged, will lead the master to spurn the restraints of interest. But what security against an abuse of power, has human wisdom ever devised which is likely to operate with such uniform and prevailing force? As Burke said of another social institution, "it makes our weakness subservient to our virtue, and grafts our benevolence, even upon our avarice." All the evidence which is accessible, the statistics of population, of consumption as shown both by imports, and the balance between production and exports, and the testimony of intelligent and candid travellers bear witness to its general efficiency. And it is to be remarked that whilst the slave partakes largely and immediately of his master's prosperity, the reverses which reduce the latter to beggary or starvation, pass almost harmless over his head. In other countries the pressure of every public calamity falls upon the working classes: but with us the slave is placed in a great measure beyond their reach, by the circumstance that his hire or ownership import a condition of life in which the means of subsistence are enjoyed. From the demoralization of extreme want, so fatal to virtue as well as happiness in other lands, he is thus always saved. It was the benevolent wish of Henry the Fourth, of France, that every peasant in his dominions might have a fowl in his pot for Sunday. In every age the patriot has offered a similar prayer for the labouring poor of his country. But it is only in the Southern States of our confederacy, that the sun ever beheld a meal of wholesome and abundant food, the daily reward of the children of toil.

The relation is so far from having any tendency to provoke those angry and resentful feelings which would excite the master to acts of cruelty, that its tendency is directly the reverse.

It was truly said by Legaré, that *parcere subjectis*, was not exclusively a Roman virtue; that it was a law of the heart, the usual attribute of undisputed power; and that there were few men who did not feel the force of that beautiful and touching appeal: "Behold, behold, I am thy servant." It was owing to this principle that when the dependence of the feudal vassal upon his lord was most complete, their mutual attachment, (as we are assured by Gilbert Stewart and other historians of this period,) was strongest, and as the feudal tenure decayed, and the law was interposed between them, the kindness upon one side and the affection and gratitude upon the other disappeared. It is not simply the consciousness of strength which tends to disarm resentment in the bosom of the master. It is the long and intimate association, connected with the feelings of interest awakened in all but the hardest hearts by the cares and responsibilities of guardianship which makes the slave an object of friendly regard, and bring him within that circle of kindly sympathies which cluster around the domestic hearth. It is a form of that generous feeling which bound the Highland chieftain to his clan, and which, with greater or less force, depending upon the virtue of the age, attaches to every relation of patriarchal authority. According to Dr. Arnold, (in his tract on the Social Condition of the Operative Classes,) the old system of English slavery was far kinder than that now existing in England of hired service. The affection between the master and the villain is shown by the fact that villainage "wore out" by voluntary manumission—a circumstance which never would have happened had the relation been one simply of profit and loss. Shakspeare in his character of old Adam, in "As You Like It," has adverted to the more genial and kindly elements which distinguished this legal service from that for wages. Orlando, in replying to the pressing entreaty of the old servant to go with him, and "do the service of a younger man in all his business and necessities," says—

"Oh good old man, how well in thee appears
The constant service of the antique world,
When service sweat for duty—not for meed."

The mutual good will of distinct classes has, in all ages, been dependent upon a well defined subordination. This opinion is confirmed by the testimony of one of the most eloquent writers of New England, in reference to the workings of its social system

as they fell under his personal observation. "I appeal," says Dana in his Essay on Law as suited to Man, "to those who remember the state of our domestic relations, when the old Scriptural terms of master and servant were in use. I do not fear contradiction when I say there was more of mutual good will then than now; more of trust on the one side and fidelity on the other; more of protection and kind care, and more of gratitude and affectionate respect in return; and because each understood well his place, actually more of a certain freedom, tempered by gentleness and by deference. From the very fact that the distinction of classes was more marked, the bond between the individuals constituting these two, was closer. As a general truth, I verily believe that, with the exception of near-blood relations, and here and there peculiar friendships, the attachment of master and servant was closer and more enduring than that of almost any other connection in life. The young of this day, under a change of fortune, will hardly live to see the eye of an old, faithful servant fill at their fall; nor will the old domestic be longer housed and warmed by the fireside of his master's child, or be followed by him to the grave. The blessed sun of those good old days has gone down, it may be for ever, and it is very cold." It is through the operation of these kindly sentiments, which it awakens on both sides, that African slavery reconciles the antagonism of classes that has elsewhere reduced the highest statesmanship to the verge of despair, and becomes the great Peace-maker of our society, converting inequalities, which are sources of danger and discord in other lands, into pledges of reciprocal service, and bonds of mutual and intimate friendship.

But a vigilant and restraining public opinion surrounds our slaves with a cumulative security. The master is no chartered libertine. Custom, the greatest of lawgivers, places visible metes and bounds upon his authority which few are so hardy as to transcend. Native humanity and Christian principle inscribe their limitations upon the living tables of his heart. A public sentiment, growing in its strength and increasing in its exactions, covers the slave with a protecting shield, far less easily or frequently broken through, than those feeble barriers of law which in our Free States, are interposed between the degraded and outcast black man, and his white bro-ther. Written laws never to be received as accurate exponents of the rights and privileges of a people, are most fallacious when appealed to as a standard, by which to determine the character of a system of slavery; for the wisest and most humane must acknowledge that the introduction of law may so disturb the harmony and good will of any domestic relation, as to breed more mischief than it can possibly cure. It is not simply in reference to the food, cloth-ing, work, holydays, punishments of slaves, that public sentiment exercises its super-vision and restraint. It looks to the whole range of their happiness and improvement. It is operating with great force in inducing masters to provide more extended facilities for their religious instruction. It has to a large extent terminated that disruption of family ties, which has always constituted the most serious obstacle to the improvement of the slave, and the severest hardship of his lot. A Scotch weaver, William Thompson, who travelled through our Southern States in 1843, on foot, sustaining himself by manual labour, and mixing constantly with our slave population, states in a book which he published on his return home, that the separation of families did not take place here to such an extent as amongst the la-bouring poor of Scotland. We know that the evil has been diminishing with every succeeding day, and I trust that public sen-timent will not leave this most beneficent work half done. The sanctity and integrity of the family union is the germ of all civ-ilization. There is nothing in slavery to make its violation inevitable. It may re-quire some time and sacrifice to accommo-date the habits of society to the universal prevalence of a permanent tenure in these relations. But through the agency of pub-lic sentiment alone, acting upon buyer and seller, and operating where necessary through combinations of benevolent neighbours, the mischief in its entire dimensions lies within the grasp of remedy.

Slavery is charged with fixing a point in the scale of civilization, beyond which it does not permit the labourer to rise. God, it is argued, has conferred the capacity and imposed the duty of improvement, but man forever denies the opportunity. I admit that the refining, elevating, and liberalizing influences of knowledge can not be impart-ed to the slave, in an equal degree with his

master. But this arises from the fact that he is a labourer, not that he is a slave. It proceeds from a combination of circumstan-ces which human laws could not alter, and which render daily toil the unavoidable por-tion of the black man. Civilization is a complex result, demanding a multitude of special offices and functions, for whose per-formance men are fitted, and even reconcil-ed by gradations in intelligence and culture. However exalting or ennobling might be the knowledge of Newton or Herschell, God in his providence has denied to the larger part of the human family, the oppor-tunity of obtaining it. The apparent hard-ship of this arrangement disappears when we reflect that this life is only a school of discipline and probation for another, and that a variety of condition involving dis-tinct spheres of duty, may be the wisest and most merciful provision for each. Every age rises to a higher level of general intelligence, but the mass of men must be satisfied with that prime wisdom, " to know that before us lies in daily life." Whilst I doubt not that,

"Through the ages one increasing purpose
  runs,
And the thoughts of men are widened with the
  circuit of the suns."

yet so long as the Divine ordinance, the poor ye have always with you, remains un-repealed—an ordinance without which the fruits of industry would be consumed, and its accumulations cease, the classes of soci-ety must be divided by a broad line of dis-parity in intellectual culture. Emancipa-tion would not relieve the slave from the necessities of daily labour, or furnish the leisure for extending mental cultivation. There might be individual exceptions; but all legislation must take its rule from the general course of human nature, not its ac-cidental departures and variations. It is emancipation and not servitude, which would forever darken and extinguish those prospects of amelioration that now lie im-aged in the bright perspective of Christian hope. The slave will partake more and more of the life-giving civilization of the master. As it is, his intimate relations with the superior race, and the unsystematic in-struction he receives in the family, have placed him in point of general intelligence above a large portion of the white labourers of Europe. It appears from the most re-cent statistics, that one half the adult population of England and Wales are unable to write their names. It was of English labourers, not American slaves, that Gray wrote those touching lines—

"But knowledge to their eyes her ample page,
Rich with the spoils of time, did ne'er unroll;
Chill penury repressed their noble rage,
And froze the genial current of the soul."

But it is supposed that our slaves can never be instructed without danger to the public safety, as knowledge, like the admission of light into a subterranean mine, might lead to an explosion. There may be circumstances in which the supreme law of self-preservation will command us to withhold from the slave the degree of information we would gladly impart. But it is never to be forgotten, that this stern and inexorable necessity will not be created by the system itself. The sin, and the responsibility of its existence will lie at the door of the misjudging philanthropy which has rashly and ignorantly interposed to adjust relations on whose balance hang great issues of liberty and civilization. If the views which have been presented are true, the more his reason was instructed, the clearer would be the slave's perception of the general equity of the arrangement which fixed his lot. But if knowledge is to introduce him to literature which will confuse his understanding by its sophistry, whilst it inflames his passions by its appeals, which will exaggerate his rights and magnify his wrongs, then mercy to the slave, as well as justice to society, require us to protect him from the folly and crime into which he might be hurried by the madness of moral intoxication. We will not throw open our gates, that the enemies of peace may sow the dragon's teeth of discord, and leave us to reap a harvest of confusion and rebellion—but when they come to plant love amongst us, to teach apostolic precepts, as elementary morality, and to hold up the standard of Holy Scripture as the rule of conduct, and proof of law, we will give them hospitable welcome.

If I have at all comprehended the elements which should enter into the determination of this momentous problem of social welfare and public authority, the existence of African Slavery amongst us, furnishes no just occasion for self-reproach; much less for the presumptuous rebuke of our fellow man. As individuals, we have cause to humble ourselves before God, for the imper-fect discharge of our duties in this, and in every other relation of life: but for its justice and morality as an element of our social polity, we may confidently appeal to those future ages, which, when the bedimming mists of passion and prejudice have vanished, will examine it in the pure light of truth, and pronounce the final sentence of impartial History. Beyond our own borders, there has been no sober and intelligent estimate of its distinctive features; no just apprehension of the nature, extent and permanence of the disparities between the races, or of the fatal consequences to the slave, of a freedom which would expose him to the unchecked selfishness of a superior civilization; no conception approaching to the reality of the power which has been exerted by a public sentiment, springing from Christian principle, and sustained by the universal instincts of self-interest, in tempering the severity of its restraints, and impressing upon it the mild character of a patriarchal relation; no rational anticipation of the improvement of which the negro would be capable under our form of servitude, if those who now nurse the wild and mischievous dream of peaceful emancipation, should lend all their energies to the maintenance of the only social system under which his progressive amelioration appears possible. African slavery is no relic of barbarism to which we cling from the ascendency of semi-civilized tastes, habits, and principles; but an adjustment of the social and political relations of the races, consistent with the purest justice, commended by the highest expediency, and sanctioned by a comprehensive and enlightened humanity. It has no doubt been sometimes abused by the base and wicked passions of our fallen nature to purposes of cruelty and wrong; but where is the school of civilization from which the stern and wholesome discipline of suffering has been banished? or the human landscape not saddened by a dark-flowing stream of sorrow? Its history when fairly written, will be its ample vindication. It has weaned a race of savages from superstition and idolatry, imparted to them a general knowledge of the precepts of the true religion, implanted in their bosom sentiments of humanity and principles of virtue, developed a taste for the arts and enjoyments of civilized life, given an unknown dignity and elevation to their type of physical, moral and intellectual man, and for two centuries during which this humanizing process has taken place, made for their subsistence and comfort, a more bountiful provision, than was ever before enjoyed in any age or country of the world by a laboring class. If tried by the test which we apply to other institutions, the whole sum of its results, there is no agency of civilization which has accomplished so much in the same time, for the happiness and advancement of our race.

I am fully persuaded, Mr. President, that the preservation of our peace and union, our property and liberty depend upon the triumph of these opinions over the delusion and ignorance which have obscured and perplexed the public judgment upon this question of slavery. I believe that they indicate the only tenable line of argument along which we can defend our rights or character. So long as men regard all forms of slavery as sinful, they will be conducted to the conclusion that any aid or comfort to them, is likewise sinful, by a logical necessity, which their passions or interests can only resist for a time. The conviction that justice is the highest expediency for the statesman, the first duty of the Christian, and should be supreme law of the State, will sooner or later establish its supremacy over all combinations of parties and interests. So long as our fellow-citizens of the North look upon this relation as barbarous and corrupting, they must and ought to desire and seek its extinction, as a great vice and crime. Every year will deepen their sympathy with the slave, suffering under unjust bonds, and inflame their resentful indignation towards the master who holds his odious property with unrelaxing grasp. Mutual self-respect is the only term of association upon which either individuals or societies can or ought to live together. How long could our Union endure, if it was to be preserved by submission to a fixed policy of injustice, and acquiescence under an accumulating burthen of reproach? We are willing to give much for Union. We will give territory for it; the broad acres we have already surrendered would make an empire. We will give blood for it; we have shed it freely upon every field of our country's danger and renown. We will give love for it; the confiding, the forgiving, the overflowing love of brothers and freemen. But much as we value it, we will not purchase it at the price of liberty or character.

A union of suspicion, aversion, injustice, in which we would be banned not blessed, outlawed not protected, whether by faction under the forms of law or revolution over them I care not, has no charms for me. The Union I love, is that which our fathers formed; a Union which, when it took its place upon the majestic theatre of history, consecrated by the benedictions of patriots and freemen, and covered all over with images of fame, was a fellowship of equal and fraternal States; a Union which was established not only as a bond of strength, but as a pledge of justice and a sacrament of affection; a Union which was intended, like the arch of the heavens, to embrace within the span of its beneficent influence all interests and sections and to rest oppressively or unequally upon none; a Union in which the North and the South—"like the double-celled heart, at every full stroke," beat the pulses of a common liberty and a common glory. Mr. Madison has recorded a beautiful incident, which occurring as the members of the Federal Convention were attaching their signatures to the Constitution, forms a fitting and significant close to its proceedings. Dr. Franklin pointing to the painting of a sun which hung behind the speaker's chair, and adverting to a difficulty which is said to exist in discriminating between the picture of a rising and a setting sun, remarked that during the progress of their deliberations, he had often looked at this painting and been doubtful as to its character, but that he now saw clearly that it was a rising sun. When the fancy of Franklin gave to the painting its auroral hues, she had dipped her pencil in his heart. Let but a healing conviction of the true character of our system of slavery enter into the public sentiment of the North; let it understand that the South is seeking to discharge, not simply the obligations of justice, but the larger debt of Christian humanity towards this degraded race; and that if it has not accomplished more, it is because its people, like the workmen upon Solomon's temple, have been compelled to labour on their social fabric with the trowel in one hand, and the sword in the other: and the old feelings of mutual regard would soon follow a mutual respect resting upon immovable foundations; the animosities and dissentions of the past would be buried in the duties of the Present and the Hopes of the Future; the memories of our great heroic age would breathe over us a second spring of patriotism: the comprehensive American sentiment which framed this league of love would revive in all its quickening power, in the bosoms of our people, spreading undivided over every portion of our territory, and operating unspent through all generations of our history; the Union would be so clasped in the North, and in the South, to our heart of hearts, that death itself could not tear loose the clinging tendrils of devotion; and that emblematic painting in which our fathers, with "no form nor feeling in their souls, unborrowed from their country," greeted with patriot prayer and hope, the rising beams of morning, would never by any line of lessening light, betoken to the eyes of their children a parting radiance.

I have an abiding faith in Time, Truth and Providence. Let but the educated mind of our society be fully awakened to the magnitude of its responsibilities, and thoroughly instructed in the duties of its mission: let it meet the falsifications of history, and perversions of philosophy, and corruptions of religion, in the varied forms of wise and temperate discussions; let it catch the spirit of Milton, when he was content to lose his sight in writing for the defence of the liberties of England, and inspired by yet deeper enthusiasm in a cause upon which may depend the liberties and civilization of the whole earth, now in common peril from a universal licentiousness of opinion, unseal all its fountains of wit, eloquence and logic; and there would soon set out from our Southern coast, a great moral Gulf Stream, able to penetrate and warm all currents of opposing thought—although they come in strength and volume of ocean tides.

—

At the close of the Annual Address, the President called Mr. Edmunds, first Vice President, to the Chair.

Mr. Newton then moved the following resolution, which was unanimously adopted:

Resolved, That the thanks of the Virginia State Agricultural Society be tendered to Professor Holcombe for the very able, eloquent and philosophical discourse which he has just delivered, and that a copy be requested for publication in all the journals of the Commonwealth, the Agricultural papers, and in the transactions of the Society.

The Chairman of the Meeting, Mr. Edmunds, stated that the Executive Committee had duly considered the subject of the practicability of uniting the two Societies, referred to them by resolution of the meeting of the 3rd instant; and that a report was in the hands of the Secretary to be now read to the meeting, if it should be their pleasure to hear it. The resolution of the 3rd instant was then read, after which the following minute, which had been adopted by the Executive Committee on the motion of Mr. Edmunds, was submitted to this meeting as their report:

"The Executive Committee of the State Agricultural Society having had under consideration the resolution of the State Society passed in general meeting on the 3rd instant, and having conferred with the Executive Committee of the Union Agricultural Society on the grave and important subject embraced in the resolution—beg leave to report unanimously, that, in the absence of a number of the members of the Committee, and in view of the deep importance of the subject, they deem it inexpedient to report prior to the next meeting of the Farmers' Assembly, upon which body the Constitution devolves the final decision."

Mr. Cox, of Chesterfield, moved the following resolution:

Resolved, That the report just presented be referred to a Committee of five, who shall have leave to retire, consider the same, and report immediately to this body, recommending such action as they may deem it proper and expedient for this meeting to adopt.

Mr. Branch proposed as a substitute the following resolution, which was accepted by the mover, and adopted by the meeting:

Resolved, That the report of the Executive Committee be recommitted, with instructions to hold further conference with the Executive Committee of the Union Agricultural Society during the time intervening, and that they report to the next meeting of the Farmers' Assembly on the practicability of a permanent union of the two

Societies, and also the terms of such union, if found practicable.

The meeting then adjourned.

FRIDAY EVENING, Nov. 5th, 1858.

The members of the Union Society of Virginia and North Carolina, and of the Virginia State Agricultural Society, convened in joint meeting at the Market Street Baptist Church to hear the Valedictory Address. Ex-President Tyler was escorted to the stand by a Committee of the two Societies, and was greeted with enthusiastic demonstrations of respect, due to the venerable statesman, who, after life-long devotion of himself to the service of his country, has so gracefully exchanged the sword of authority for the ploughshare and the pruning-hook, and surrendered the robes and the tenure of office for the simple vesture and the dignified retirement of the citizen Farmer. He then proceeded to deliver the following Valedictory:

Mr. President and Gentlemen:

My task is readily accomplished. I am here to congratulate you on the continued success of the Society which bears the name of our time-honoured Commonwealth, and of that with which it has upon this occasion united its destinies. That success is strikingly illustrated by the evidences presented on those grounds. The earth, although parched and dried up by a drought of unusual duration, has nevertheless contributed its cereals, and fruits, and flowers, to embellish the scene of your Fair Grounds, while your mines, now in a course of rapid and successful development, have given up specimens of their hidden treasures, in proof of vast resources yet to be dug from the bosom of distant mountains. The manufacturer on his part has been no listless spectator of the passing scene. The results of the loom and the spindle—of the ingenious contrivances to mitigate the severity of labour—of improvements in the mechanic arts—of the numberless machines, apparently instinct with life, so admirably and systematically do they perform their functions—all bespeak that hand and mind are alike at work, and that our fellow-citizens are every where actively engaged in aiding the good part of raising food for the hungry, and clothes for the naked, and in ameliorating the condition of society in all its departments. Here, too, have been exhibited the products of your pastures and fields—in horses matchless for blood and strength—in cattle of the finest form and structure—of sheep admirable for flesh and fleece, and of other animals which contribute so essentially to the comforts and necessities of life; and here, too, the Dairy and Poultry-yard have liberally contributed their stores in order to enrich the scenes. May I not, then, congratulate you on this sixth times repeated success of your patriotic associations. The opinion has extensively prevailed in other States that Virginia had seen her best days; that her soil, by a long and severe course of tillage, was exhausted, and that her people led a torpid existence, content to pass their lives in dreams of other days, and in the boast of an illustrious ancestry, and in anticipation of a future that can never come to an idle and effeminate race. Bid these mistaken revilers visit the Fair Grounds of the numerous Agricultural Societies throughout the State. If this does not answer to dispel the delusion, take them to your several estates throughout the broad surface of the country; point out to them the march of improvement within the period of twenty years; shew them your fields during the season of harvest home, teeming with the golden abundance; tell them that those fields now producing from twenty to forty fold, were indeed then worn and nearly exhausted by a culture of 250 years; say to them what was truly the case, that our people had to abandon the lands on which they were born, to flee to others embosomed in the distant wilderness, where ploughman's whistle had never been heard, or woodman's axe had never resounded since the days of the great flood. That in deserting their old paternal homesteads, where they had passed the days of their infancy and early manhood, they might well break out in the language of Melibeus to Tityrus when forced to leave Italy—

"Nos patriæ fines, et dulcia linquimus arva;
Nos patriam fugimus:"

But that now the broom-straw old fields had disappeared—migration had nearly ceased, and that the old homesteads were ample and broad enough to shelter one and all, and the lands restored to more than their primeval fertility. If not yet satisfied, transport them to regions but recently visited by the steam-engine, and open to their view extensive and fertile districts which, until now, have been alien to the world, and almost buried in primeval forests. Tell them that the hum of industry already disturbs the silence which there has ruled supreme, and that in a few years more the voice of activity and life will awaken the one universal echo through mountain and vale. And if still unconvinced, carry the unbelievers into your workshops and your mines. Point out to them the increase of the mechanical arts, and exhibit to them the extent of your mineral treasures—carry them, if no farther, to the banks of the Holstein, and call their attention to a comparatively small area of valley and mountain, whose treasures of salt and plaster exceed in value the estimated value of the great and overshadowing city of New York. If, with these evidences of increasing prosperity, they alter into the nasal twang, which I have often heard, of a decline of intellect among us, lead them into an assembly of our farmers, and after having heard their debates, then may we exclaim in an exultant voice, these are our people, and here are the men whose fathers were in the olden time the leaders of the hosts to the land of promise, and are themselves worthy to be their successors—and to finish the picture, then point them to your wives and mothers, leading by their hands their infant children, to swear upon the altar of the living God eternal enmity, not as Hannibal, the Carthagenian, against an earthly power, but against immorality and vice in all its forms. Such is Virginia now, and such the symbol of a still greater Virginia that is to be. These make her what she is, the great conservative State of the Union, and impart to her a moral influence more important than is to be found in numbers, or in an army with banners.

Need I do more than point you to the motto of that glorious flag which floated over our fathers in other days, and has waved over you on this occasion. Let the motto of each and all be *Perseverando.* And where can that old flag more proudly float than over that city which, by its heroism and its perseverance, has sought every field on which honor was to be won, and has gloriously acquired the title of the Cockade city of Virginia, "the blessed mother of us all." I remember well the day when the cry came from the far northwest for aid and succour. Discomfiture had befallen our arms, and a combined force pressed upon our exposed frontiers. Then there stepped forth from the ranks of her citizens, that noble and gallant corps which, with a step firm and determined, entered the wilderness and breasted at Fort Meigs, the wild and furious assaults of Proctor and its hosts. Nor can I quit this theme without expressing your sense, Mr. President, and that of those assembled here at the manner of your reception by the citizens of this flourishing city upon the present occasion. Petersburg has interwoven an additional wreath into her cockade, and there it floats in all the enticing loveliness of hospitality—unbounded and unlimited. Wear in your heart of hearts gentlemen, that proud old motto, " *Perseverando*. Let no petty local jealousies introduce discord into your councils. For men to differ is the inevitable result of freedom of thought and of speech—let no such differences affect the great and valuable association which you have so successfully organized. It is Virginia that pleads— you Mr. President of the State Agricultural Society, permit me to say, are more than all others interested in this. Through your analysis of soils, I speak what I think, Virginia has been materially aided in being what she is. The existence of the State Agricultural Society is materially due to your labours. Proud and lofty is the monument. Shall we not preserve it undefiled and unmutilated? Bring up your offerings to the next annual Fair. Let your wives bring also theirs, and your children theirs. Let the last bring garlands woven of the bright flowers of the forest, and the field, and the garden. They will be fit emblems of their own purity, and types of their own brightness and beauty.

At the close of the address, on motion of the President,

Resolved, That the thanks of the Societies be tendered to Ex-President Tyler for the feeling and appropriate manner in which he has addressed the meeting, and that he be requested to furnish a copy of his discourse for publication.

The President reminded the Societies that, as the occasion was one of congratulation and of leave-taking after having enjoyed a delightful season of re-union and social intercourse, while witnessing one of the most successful exhibitions ever held in Virginia, any member present would be gladly heard who had any remarks to make, deemed appropriate to the occasion.

Messrs. Charles Carter Lee, James A. Seddon and Willoughby Newton, each delivered appropriate addresses in answer to calls made upon them by the meeting.

And then with the kindest feelings, and with fraternal harmony, the meeting adjourned.   CH. B. WILLIAMS, *Sec'y*.

For the Planter.

Profitable Treatment of an Orchard.

A. A. Campbell's annual contribution to the Nottoway Agricultural Club.

MR. PRESIDENT:

Early in the month of March 1857, I had my apple orchard, containing three and a half acres of land, broken up with a two horse plough, say six or seven inches deep. This lot had been kept for eight years as a grazing lot, during which time a strong sod of wire and other grasses had formed on it; it was cross-plowed, and the heavy drag immediately passed over it; in which situation it was permitted to remain until the 28th, when the harrows were again passed over it, leaving it in fine tilth : the land was in good heart, though not rich. It was then laid off in rows, seven feet apart, with a trowel hoe, and planted in an early variety of corn, brought from the mountains, $2\frac{1}{2}$ feet in the row, two stalks in the hill—and no manure of any kind was used. Between the first and tenth of May, a trowel hoe furrow was run midway between the corn rows, say $3\frac{1}{2}$ feet from the corn and the land planted in the corn-field peas. This piece of land was selected more with the view of benefitting my orchard than the expectation of receiving a remunerating return for my labour. The subsequent cultivation was with the harrows and two hoe workings, all done in good time.

During the last week in July following, I had a three-tooth harrow run between the corn and pea rows; opened a drill with a trowel hoe plough and sowed in the furrows Reese's Manipulated Guano, at the rate of 200 pounds per acre, and immediately followed on with a well constructed Turnip drill, which deposited the turnip seed to my entire satisfaction; at the same time partially incorporating the guano with the loose earth in the drill, by the action of the spout through which the seed pass. The seed were readily covered by an iron tooth garden rake and the operation finished, with but little labour. The subsequent cultivation was only one hoe working at the time of thinning the turnips, which were left in the drill from six to ten inches apart.

As soon as the corn began to get out of the milk state, I commenced cutting down and throwing it to my stock hogs, after having stripped off the blades of as much as would last the hogs three or four days; thus saving a good stack of fodder and giving the turnips more sun and air, and cutting off the draught on the land. My hogs did well on this feed.

It is impossible to say what the land would have produced in corn if it had been permitted to stand until matured. I suppose it would have produced five or six barrels to the acre, my opinion was corroborated by others who saw it. The crop of peas was a beautiful one, supplying a large family abundantly during the season, with that most wholesome and nutritious vegetable, aud in fall affording a good supply of seed peas. After gathering the dried peas, the vines were cut off with tobacco knives, cured and stacked for the stock in winter; they were eaten greedily by cows and sheep.

It only remains to say something of the turnip crop. It will be recollected, by the Club, that the last was an unfavorable year in this county for this crop; the fly and grasshoppers were unusually destructive, notwithstanding which I raised a good crop for the land and season; most of the turnips were large and well-flavoured. The crop was not measured otherwise than by the cart load; and estimating the cart load at twenty-five bushels, the crop amounted to about 300 bushels; these were put up in mounds and covered over with corn-stalks and earth, and have been beneficially fed to my stock during the winter and spring months,—they kept well until the cold spell in March when they rotted badly.

On the 5th day of October 1857, the land having been previously cleared of the corn and peas—the turnips still remaining on the land—was sowed in wheat, at the rate of $1\frac{1}{2}$ bushels per acre, and 200 pounds of well-mixed and thoroughly incorporated Mexican and Icabo guanos, (done in my own guano-house, under my supervision,) in equal quantities by weight, and thoroughly harrowed in. Around and between the turnips the wheat was chopped in with hand hoes. The turnips were gathered by hand in December. The wheat came up evenly and regularly, and is at this time (April 27th) a beautiful and promising lot, comparing favorably with my tobacco lots, from which a fine crop is expected if no casualty befals it.

A. A. CAMPBELL.

Specific Manures, &c.

Experiments by W. J. Harris, reported to the Nottoway Club.

MR. PRESIDENT :—An analysis of Tobacco by Mr. W. A. Shepard, of Randolph Macon College, which appeared in a late number of the Planter, agrees so well with some experiments made by me, that I think it will prove a safe guide in the application of specific manures for Tobacco. Not being able to make as much good farm-yard manure or compost as would be necessary for a crop, I have been compelled to make up the deficiency with guano, applied jointly with them, or alone. When guano was used alone, unless the land was very good, the crop always failed to fulfill what might reasonably have been expected from its early growth. It would start off finely and reach a large size, but as soon as the maturing process commenced it begun to *burn* at the bottom, or *fire* at the top; or, if it escaped these disasters, it ripened, or rather dried up, thin and poor. It was evident, therefore, that, although the guano could give it size, it could not ripen it properly. As guano contained very little potash, and Tobacco a great deal, and as wood ashes is known to be one of the best manures for Tobacco, it appeared clear to me that potash and lime, when needed, would supply the deficiency.

The first experiment I made was on a piece of thin, worn-out land, on which I applied a dressing of oak leaves and lime, saltpetre and guano. The oak leaves and lime were applied about two months before the saltpetre and guano. The result was, that I believe I got a better crop than from an ordinary dressing of stable manure. The next experiment was made with saltpetre and salt, and a small quantity of leached ashes—broadcast, and guano in the drill, which made the richest and heaviest Tobacco I ever made from any application. The land on which this was made was a stiff red clay, and probably contained a sufficient quantity of lime. The first was a very poor sandy soil.

Mr. Shepard's analysis shows a very large quantity of potash and lime in both the dried leaf and stalk,—as much as 6 pounds to the 100 pounds; so that an acre of land, to produce 1000 pounds of leaf and 200 pounds of stalk, would have to supply 72 pounds of potash and 72 pounds of lime, —the two making two-thirds of the inorganic elements of the plant.

Salt is no doubt very beneficial as the analysis shows a large per cent. of chlorine and soda. Without being guided by an analysis I had, in the above mixture, everything of importance the analysis calls for. The guano furnished the nitrogen and phosphoric acid to give the growth—the ashes and saltpetre to furnish potash, and salt the chlorine and soda.

From the very large proportion of potash and lime in a well matured leaf and stalk of Tobacco, I think it very probable that a deficiency of these alkalies prevents a proper maturing of the leaf, and brings on *burning, fire* and *starvation*—(to both leaf and planter.)

Saltpetre,	30 to 40 lbs.,	
Ashes,	quantum habet,	Per acre.
Salt,	2 bushels,	
Guano,	200 lbs.,	

Respectfully submitted.

WM. J. HARRIS.

Experiments with Peruvian and Columbian Guano, both Separate and Mixed.

Report of W. R. Bland to the Nottoway Club.

I last fall, about the 12th of October, sowed one and a half acres of land in wheat, dressed with 250 pounds of Columbian guano, at a cost of $5 62½, one acre and a half dressed with 212 pounds Peruvian guano at a cost of $5 72, and six acres dressed with a mixture of the two guanos, 550 pounds Columbian and 370 pounds Peruvian, at a cost of $22 37. The acre and a half dressed with Columbian guano produced five shocks wheat, estimated at two bushels per shock, giving ten bushels, or six and two-third bushels per acre, cost $5 62, product at $1 50 per bushel $15 00, profit $9 37; profit per acre $6 25. The acre and a half dressed with Peruvian guano produced five shocks wheat, estimated at three bushels per shock, gives fifteen bushels, or ten bushels per acre; cost of guano $5 72, 15 bushels wheat, at $1 50, $22 50, profit $16 78, or a profit of $11 18⅔ per acre. The six acres dressed with a mixture of the two guanos, at a cost of $22 37, produced twenty-four shocks, which, at three bushels per shock, gives seventy-two bushels, which, at $1 50, gives $108; profit $85 63, or a profit of $14 40⅝ per acre.

The three sections of land were of as nearly equal fertility as I could well get, all very poor. If there was any difference, the land on which the separate applications were made was rather the best. The wheat was, I believe, all sown the same day.

       · WM. R. BLAND.

July 9th, 1857.

Comparative Experiment with Peruvian Guano and Reese's Manipulated Guano.

Reported to the Nottoway Club by T. F. Epes.

On my tobacco lot last year, I tried Peruvian guano on one half, and Reese's Manipulated Guano on the other. That on which the Peruvian guano was applied grew off best. It was topped at ten and twelve leaves. The other was topped at ten and eight. It was most leafy and ripened thicker. Whether attributable to the lower topping or Manipulated Guano I don't know.   T. F. EPES.

May, 1858.

Experiments to Substitute Peruvian Guano (in part) on the Wheat Crop.

Report of Travis H. Epes to the Nottoway Club.

Last fall, Peruvian guano being high, I used 100 pounds of it to the acre on wheat mixed with 50 pounds of Mexican and 50 of Jordan's Superphosphate of Lime. All of the wheat that was seeded before the heavy rain of the first of November looks very well, and is as good (except being a little too thin) as when the same land was in wheat, with 200 pounds of Peruvian guano to the acre. That seeded after the rain looks well and healthy also, and the whole crop is said by many farmers to be the best they have seen.

Respectfully submitted.

       TRAVIS H. EPES.

Those who are in the power of evil habits must conquer them as they can; and conquered they must be, or neither wisdom nor happiness can be attained.—*Johnson.*

Toilet Soap.

Take 6 lbs. White soap,
    1½ lbs. Sal Soda,
    1 table-spoonful Spirits Turpentine,
    ½   "   Hartshorn,
    1½ gallons of water.

JELLY SOAP.

24 ozs. water, or 1½ pints,
    1 oz. Shaving Soap,
    1½ ozs Carb. Soda,
    10 grains Pulv. Borax,
    5   "   "   Ammonia,
    1½ drachms Spirits Turpentine.

Boil the water and mix the materials well.

The above recipe is taken from an old newspaper, and it is thought to be identical with the celebrated Roraback recipe which is offered for sale all over the country.* It is said the Roraback Soap yields upon analysis nearly 40 per cent. of tallow. This agrees very well with the above recipe, for the common White Soap yields 70 per cent. of tallow. The usual colouring matter of soap, is vermillion.   SCHEELE.

       [*Independent Blade.*

MR. EDITOR :—You will confer a favour upon one of the readers of the Journal, by publishing the above. By a perusal of it, the Rorabacks can ascertain whether they have been sold or not. It may or may not be correct, but it will do no harm to put people on their guard. Every eight or ten years a sort of soap paroxism convulses the country. Washing made easy, and soap made cheaper than Paddy's brooms, are all the go. All the scientific skill of chemistry has long since been spent upon this vexed question, and soap is still nothing more than the union of an oil and an alkali—call it what you may. The firm white soaps are chiefly made of the olive oil and carbonate soda, common salt being added to promote the granulation and perfect separation of the soap. It is marbled by stirring in a solution of sulp. iron. Common household soaps are made mainly of soda and tallow; or if potash is used, salt is added to harden it. Yellow soap is made by the addition of rosin. Common soft soap is made from potash and any oily substance, or a strong lye made from ashes and any animal oil—the lye is much improved by the addition of

---

       * It is not.—ED. F. & P.

lime to the ash hopper—but soap, made as it may be, must consist of an oil and an alkali.

A considerable stir has been made lately in New York, by developement of the fact in the Supreme Court, that the "Balm of a Thousand Flowers" was nothing but good soap; that it was compounded of greese, lye, sugar and alcohol, dignified with the name of palm oil, potash, &c.

Certainly it must be a money-making business—ten dollars a gallon for an article which can be manufactured for six cents a gallon. So much for a fancy name. "Old women," save your soap grease—fancy detergents are looking up. Give a big name. Call it Mirangipania Humbugifolia, and advertise 1000 certificates from the afflicted, and your fortune is made.

But talking of soapsuds—take one gallon of water, pound of washing soda, and a quarter of a pound of unslacked lime, put them in water and simmer twenty minutes; when cool, pour off the clear fluid into glass or stone ware, (it will ruin earthenware.) Put your clothes in, soak over night, wring them out in the morning, and put them into the wash kettle, with enough water to cover them. To a common sized kettle put a tea-cup full of the fluid; boil half an hour, then wash well through one suds, and rinse thoroughly in two waters, and if you don't give up you are paid for your trouble, I'm mistaken.—*Independent Blade.*

A Fair and Happy Milkmaid

Is a country wench, that is so far from making herself beautiful by art, that one look of her is able to put all face-physic out of countenance. She knows a fair look is but a dumb orator to commend virtue, therefore minds it not. All her excellencies stand in her so silently, as if they had stolen upon her without her knowledge. The lining of her apparel, which is herself, is far better than outsides of tissue; for though she be not arrayed in the spoil of the silkworm, she is decked in innocence, a far better wearing. She doth not, with lying long in bed, spoil both her complexion and conditions: nature hath taught her, too, immoderate sleep is rust to the soul; she rises therefore with Chanticlere, her dame's cock, and at night makes the lamb her curfew. In milking a cow, and straining the teats through her fingers, it seems that so sweet a milk-press makes the milk whiter or sweeter; for never came almond-gore or aromatic ointment on her palm to taint it. The golden ears of corn fall and kiss her feet when she reaps them, as if they wished to be bound and lead prisoners by the same hand that felled them. Her breath is her own, which scents all the year long of June, like a new-made hay-cock. She makes her hand hard with labour, and her heart soft with pity; and when winter evenings fall early, sitting at her merry wheel, she sings defiance to the giddy wheel of fortune. She doth all things with so sweet a grace, it seems ignorance will not suffer her to do ill, being her mind is to do well. She bestows her year's wages at next fair, and in choosing her garments, counts no bravery in the world like decency. The garden and bee-hive are all her physic and surgery, and she lives the longer for it. She dares go alone and unfold sheep in the night, and fears no manner of ill, because she means none; yet to say truth, she is never alone, but is still accompanied with old songs, honest thoughts, and prayers, but short ones; yet they have their efficacy, in that they are palled with ensuing idle cogitations. Lastly, her dreams are so chaste, that she dare tell them; only a Friday's dream is all her superstition; that she conceals for fear of anger. Thus lives she, and all her care is, she may die in the spring-time, to have store of flowers stuck upon her winding-sheet.—*Overbury.*

Benevolence.

When thou considerest thy wants, when thou beholdest thy imperfections, acknowledge his goodness, O Man! who honoured thee with reason, endowed thee with speech, and placed thee in society to receive and confer reciprocal helps and mutual obligations.

Thy food, thy clothing, thy convenience of habitation, thy protection from the injuries, thy enjoyment of the comforts and the pleasures of life, thou owest to the assistance of others, and couldest not enjoy but in the bands of society. It is thy duty, therefore, to be friendly to mankind, as it is thy interest that men should be friendly to thee.

As the rose breatheth sweetness from its own nature, so the heart of a benevolent man produceth good works.—*Dodsley.*

SILESIAN EWES.

The above engraving represents a group of Silesian Ewes, exhibited at the late State Fair at Petersburg, by S. S. Bradford, Esq., of Culpeper.

Mr. B. has lately purchased largely of this variety of fine wool sheep from the celebrated flocks of George Campbell of Vermont, and William Chamberlain of New York. These gentlemen, by careful breeding and judicious management, have now, it is said, as pure blooded flocks as are to be found in this country. Indeed, such is their high character for purity, that orders are annually received by their owners from Ohio, Pennsylvania, Kentucky, Michigan, California, Texas, and even from Buenos Ayres.

These sheep are hardy and easily kept, producing short wool, but of very fine staple, which is highly valued by the manufacturer.

This group attracted great admiration at the Fair, and were considered equal to any specimen of fine wools ever exhibited in Virginia.

The introduction of wool-growing in Eastern Virginia has been but partial, and the experiments in sheep-husbandry not always satisfactory. The fine wool sheep introduced have been chiefly of the Saxon variety, which, while distinguished for their fineness of fleece, have been liable to the strong objection of weak constitutions, and the unusual mortality consequent upon that infirmity, heightened by the neglect which too generally prevailed of allowing them indifferent and insufficient food, and leaving them exposed to the inclemency of winter without the protection of any kind of shelter. Of course they were unprofitable, both for "flesh and fleece." Mr. Bradford was not discouraged by these disadvantages. He resolved to persevere in his efforts to improve the character of his flock, giving special attention to those points in which he saw its deficiencies. He believed that a hardier race might be produced, which, by proper attention, would repay the expense of their keep, even upon a much more liberal scale of expenditure than had yet been essayed.

In pursuance of these views he sent to Germany and procured a regularly disciplined and experienced shepherd. He purchased of Mr. Campbell and other good flock masters in Vermont, some pure blooded Spanish Merinos, brought them to Virginia and gave them good feed and shelter and careful attention. Very soon the improvement both of his flock and of his farm, began to attract the attention of his neighbors, and Mr. Bradford found himself in receipt of a handsome income from the produce of his flock.

When some years ago he introduced sheep upon his farm, Mr. B. says it was in a very exhausted, naked, and unproductive condition; now his pastures are thickly coated with fine sward, and his cultivated fields yield him more wheat and corn than when the whole farm was appropriated to the production of these cereals. Although his land has been greatly enhanced in value by thorough under-drainage of all the low grounds, by very deep ploughing and a general system of good culture, yet, he thinks his flock of sheep has enabled him to increase the general productiveness of his farm much more rapidly than he could possibly have done by any other system. Mr. B. has good warm, dry shelters for his sheep; during winter they are every night and morning fed under these, in racks and troughs, so constructed as to prevent any considerable loss of hay and other food. These sheds are kept well littered with straw, leaves or other coarse material most easily obtained, and once or twice a week are dusted with plaster, and occasionally with a sprinkling of crushed bones, which greatly improves the value of the manure. During summer the sheep are housed of cold wet nights, and at any time while raining, and never turned out to grass of mornings until the dew is off the grass,—eating of dewy or frozen grass, and exposure to wet weather, being considered injurious to their health. In all good weather of summer, his sheep sleep out on the fields in light, portable hurdles. During this season, his shepherd, with his dog and gun, sleeps by the flock in a small house on wheels, which by means of a yoke of steers, is moved along with the sheep fold, and enables him perfectly to protect the sheep against the trespasses of dogs and thieves.

As soon as the oat crop is removed, the flock is turned on the stubble to sleep, selecting the thinnest portions, until it is all ploughed and seeded down in wheat—during this period of between two and three months, a flock of 1,000 sheep, will sleep over some 25 or 30 acres, and will fertilize them as well, Mr. B. thinks, for the production of the wheat crop, as an application of 200 pounds guano per acre, and much better and more permanently for the ensuing grass crop. Under this system, it is obvious that wool-growing can not be unprofitable. The average yield of his flock, Mr. B. says, is from 4½ to 5 pounds of washed wool, which usually finds ready sale at about 50 cents per pound.

In the old wool-growing States, where sheep receive proper attention, and the utmost care and judgment are exercised in selection and breeding, there are choice flocks which yield annually an average of 6 pounds, and a few as high as 7 pounds of washed wool.

In endeavoring to obtain as large a yield of wool as is practicable, regard must be had to good condition as well as to blood— for sheep, like other animals, other things being equal, remunerate their owners in proportion to the care bestowed upon them; wool will not grow while the animal has food sufficient only to keep it in a breathing condition—the demands of vitality must first be supplied, and it is only by increasing the food beyond this point that we can hope to realize a profit from wool or flesh; even in the pure Merino of different folds, the amount of wool would vary considerably, accordingly as they had been well or badly kept and bred in years past. The proportion, too, of lambs reared, varies greatly in different years, under different treatment. Mortality amongst them is frequently very great when neglected in cold wet seasons; the ordinary loss is perhaps as high as 15 or 20 per cent; but this can be greatly reduced by a provision of wholesome and nutritious food and warm dry shelters, with careful attention during lambing season. There is no reason in nature, Mr. B. thinks, why there should be a greater mortality with them than with calves and pigs, and one explanation of ordinary mortality may usually be found in the neglect or mismanagement of the breeder. It is a law of nature that animals require nutrition in proportion to their natural weight of carcass, but no animal known to the economy of our agriculture can be maintained with so much ease and so little expense as the Merino sheep; nor is there any in which there is so little waste and so little loss. They will thrive on tracts where neat cattle would starve. Bushes, briars, and coarse herbage, which infest our lands, are extirpated by them, and white clover, blue grass and green sward rapidly introduced. The continued pressure of their feet consolidates without penetrating the earth, and the uniform dropping of their liquid and solid excrements over its surface maintains the land in constant progression in fertility and value. The extent of profit to be derived from wool-growing depends much, of course, upon the scale in the prices of wool, as well as the kind of sheep and the condition in which they are kept; but our observation satisfies us that even at the present comparatively low prices, few occupations can be more remunerative or attractive to the farmer than raising fine wool and sheep.

For the Southern Planter.

Facts for the Curious; or Remarkable Peculiarities of Four Cows.

I have intended, Mr. Editor, for some time, to make public, through your columns, the remarkable facts which have occurred, under my own observation, in relation to four cows, the history of which I am about to narrate. Some of these facts are so strange, as almost to overleap the bounds of credibility, yet I shall give them, under the sanction of my own name, and hold myself responsible for their truth. As truth is sometimes stranger than fiction, it only *proves* that the silent workings of Providence are often far beyond the utmost contrivings of man.

But to the facts proposed. Some years ago, I had a very good milch cow, of the scrub breed, whose constant habit it was, to give milk literally, from calf to calf, without cessation. On one occasion, I remember distinctly, to have seen her give *good, white milk*, at night, and in the morning ensuing, she had a calf; and so continued on. One striking effect of this habit of hers was, that her calves were always small and poor. But independent of that, I esteemed her very much, for she was always " Charley at the rack." So much for the first fact. Now for the second. Some few years ago, I had a Short Horn Durham cow, that after having a calf or two, appeared to be with calf again; and observing one evening when the cattle were penned, that she was suffering very much from the great distention of her udder, I very naturally supposed that she had calved, and had hid the calf in the pasture; and had been driven up without it.— In the morning, I directed a servant to drive her to the pasture, and bring her back, with the calf. He drove her to the pasture as directed, but after a while returned, saying that the cow showed no disposition to go to the calf; that he had searched the field, but could find none. I directed him to take the dogs to the field and set them after her, knowing, that instinct, would cause her to run directly to the calf, if it was hid. He returned again however, with no better success than before. I then had the cow milked, supposing that she had lost the calf by some casualty; and that in a short time I should see the buzzards after it. I watched for some days, but saw no sign of the supposed lost calf. Well, here was a mystery I could not solve, so I pocketed it, but had no satisfactory solution of it until the expiration of five years; and here it is. The cow gave her usual quantity of milk for 18 months, (which is the usual time all my cows milk between their calves,) when she was turned dry to calve again. This she did in due time, bearing a female calf, which I now own. At three years old, this calf, now a heifer, also appeared to be with calf; but when the time came to calve, she also had none. So I was compelled to have her milked, to keep her bag from spoiling. This brought back fresh to my memory the conduct of her mother, but only tended to increase the mystery. For, although I have a great fondness for stock, and have read every thing that I could lay my hand on, published either in this country or Europe, I had never seen, heard, nor read of a cow that had come to her milk, but from having a calf, or some other exciting cause. So I stuck a peg there, and determined, if I ever had another opportunity of observing, to put the matter beyond all cavil. In due course of time she was bulled, and again appeared to be pregnant.

On closely observing my other cattle, I found another heifer that I thought would calve about the same time, so I had them turned into my yard to keep each other company, in their state of family solicitude, where I might have a full opportunity of watching the denouement. In due time the other heifer had a calf, but still the *inexplicable* held on, until it became apparent that her bag would certainly spoil unless I had her milked, which was accordingly done.— Not until then was the mystery entirely solved. I had read of cases in the medical books, of women having false conceptions, and passing what is called a *mole*; but this cow had no appearance of having passed any thing of that sort. So much for the third fact.

And now for the fourth. Some years ago, I happened in Lynchburg, Va., and on meeting with my old friend, Mr. John M. Warrick, we soon got into a conversation on the subject of improved stock; and at his request, I rode out with him to his farm, to see his herd of Durhams. After pointing out to me several fine animals, he called my attention to a pair of twin heifers, then about two years old, with very large udders. I asked him if they had not been bulled; he said they had not. I remarked to him that they evidently had milk in their bags, and requested him to have one of them driven to his lot in town and regularly milked, which he readily promised to do. He asked me if I had ever known a heifer to give milk under similar circumstances. I replied I had not, but that I once had a yearling heifer that was kept in my orchard, with some young calves, and one of them brought her to her milk by repeatedly sucking her, and I had somewhere read of a case of an old grandmother who had not borne a child for many years, having been brought to her milk again by taking a motherless child to sleep with her, and giving it the breast to keep it quiet.

The next time I saw Mr. Warrick, he informed me that he had the heifer milked for some time, and finally wishing to breed from her, he had turned her dry.

While upon the subject of cows, it may be proper that I should give some explanation of an incidental remark I made in the first part of this communication—which was that all my cows milked about eighteen months between their calves. Some thirty years ago, I observed that my cows that had annual calves were not worth half as much at the pail as those that intermitted a year. So I determined to correct it, by killing off and selling all the annual breeders. So that now, and for many years past, I have had no cows in my herd of that description.— This, in part, gave rise to another practice of mine, which is different from my neighbours. It is this: I always have cows at the pail, (whose calves had been weaned,) to give milk at night. This makes it convenient and profitable, to let the young calves run with their mothers in the day, and take all the milk in the morning. By this method, the cows and calves are kept quiet all day. I get as much milk, and the calves grow off more thriftily, and are consequently much better prepared to stand the first winter. It always distressed me to ride by a house on a long summer day, and find the cows *lowing* at the fence, and the poor little calves on the other side, in feebler accents, proclaiming the cruelty of their owners. R. J. GAINES.

Charlotte County, Dec. 21, 1858.

P. S.—At some future time, Mr. Editor, if I can overcome my great aversion to writing, I should like to give you some experiments I have been making, in the improvement of worn out land, by the repeated applications of guano alone. R. J. G..

[We shall feel very much obliged if our esteemed correspondent will overcome his aversion to writing, and will favor our readers with the result of his experience in the important work of reclaiming exhausted lands—a subject of almost universal interest to the readers of the *Planter*.—EDITOR.]

For the Southern Planter.

Lard Cured with Soda.

Mr. Editor—I find on page 690 of the November number of the *Southern Planter*, in an article on "Curing Lard with Soda," the following sentence: "To every gallon of lard, before it is washed, put one ounce of sal soda, dissolved in one gil of water; the fat needs no other washing or soaking than that just before being put on to cook."

Please let me know what is meant—must the sal soda be put in and then washed out? or must the fat be washed and the soda put with it in the pot.

You will oblige more than one of your subscribers by complying with the above request. Respectfully, W.

We have seen but one specimen of lard cured by the recipe referred to. That was beautifully white, and as nice as it could be. The fat was washed to free it from blood, &c., *before* it was put on to boil, and the soda was mixed with water according to the proportions directed by the recipe in our November number, and stirred into the pot of fat only half full, after it was hung over the fire.

We suppose that the chief benefit derived from the soda is the neutralization of some one, or all, of the acids probably evolved in the process of boiling, and of which there are three, viz: margaric, oleic and stearic. Certainly lard cured after this formulary is whiter, and nicer than any other we have ever seen.

For the Southern Planter.

Is the Cultivation of Oats in an Orchard Injurious to Peach Trees?

GLOUCESTER, Nov. 29, 1858.

Mr. Editor—I am anxious to obtain some information on the subject of the treatment of the Peach tree, and would be grateful if you will answer some questions.

Do you know of any reason why oats should be injurious to a peach orchard?—Some of my neighbours have advised me against cultivating oats in my orchard, and have given as a reason that it would ruin it. I have, with considerable trouble and expense, raised a fine orchard of choice fruit, and would dislike to injure it.

Do you know of any instance where the plan has been pursued with injury or otherwise? My plan was to sow oats, and turn the hogs in as soon as they were ripe, which would be in time for the peaches as they commenced falling.

I saw some time since in your paper, or the "Farmer," I do not recollect which, that a solution of potash, strong enough to bear an egg, was the best wash for the body of the tree. Have you ever tried it, or do you know any body who has? When should it be applied? Have you ever tried the plan of drawing the earth away from the roots of the tree, to destroy the worms? Does it answer, and if so, how long should the roots be exposed, and how much of them? By answering the above queries, you will much oblige a subscriber.

W. F. JONES.

———

SOUTHERN GREENWOOD NURSERY, }
Richmond, Va., Dec. 21, 1858. }

Mr. Editor—In reply to the inquiries made by Mr. W. F. Jones, relative to the treatment of fruit trees, I can say, that I have known several instances where persons have planted good, thrifty, fruit trees in November, or early in the Spring, then sowed the ground with oats, and by the time it was matured, the trees were nearly all dead, owing, in my opinion, to the obstruction of a free circulation of air, and the atmosphere being filled with something exhaled by the oats while in a growing state, which is instantly absorbed by the tree acting as a poison thereto; yet at present it is difficult to say what *that something* is, I only *know such to be facts*, while trees planted under the same circumstances, except that the ground was cultivated in peas and potatoes, become healthy and vigorous. I have also known instances, where the cultivation of oats in orchards of more advanced age has had similar effects, though not so instantly fatal. I would recommend the entire prohibition of all crops in an orchard, except peas, potatoes, or cabbage, and in some instances, tobacco. I have been using strong soap-suds as a wash for the bodies of fruit trees for the last fifteen years, and from the advantageous results arising therefrom, I most *heartily recommend* it as superior to any other for that purpose. This should be applied with a coarse cloth during the growing season, viz: May, July, and the latter part of August.

By observation and experience, I have found it very essential to the health, vigour, and longevity of the peach tree, that the earth be taken from the body during the months of Dec'r, Jan'ry and February, thus exposing the top of the main roots from two to six inches, according to the size of the tree, after which, take all remaining insects from the body and roots with a knife or chisel, and throw upon them a half peck of leached ashes, or a small quantity of lime, previous to returning the top soil.

By a strict adherence to the above suggestions, trees can be made to retain a thrifty and fruitful condition to an advanced age.   Yours, truly,

LEWIS TUDOR.

———

Quantity and Value of the Manure of Cattle.

Since the publication of our article on this subject (Co. Gent. of March 5th, and Cult. of April), we have found the following remarks in the report of a recent discussion at a meeting of the London Farmers' Club, England. The gentleman who opened the discussion, Mr. Baker, is reported to have said that he had found, on investigation, that a cow feeding on 100 lbs of grass gave 71 lbs of solid and liquid deposit. An ox would produce 1¼ cwt. while feeding on turnips or mangold wurtzel with 24 to 28 lbs. of solid straw daily; or, in all, about 150 lbs. of solid and liquid manure would be produced by an ox daily. (This, we presume, is true only of an ox of very large size, and weighing about 2000 lbs.) An ox, if kept feeding continually on turnips, grain, and hay, in the ordinary mode, would produce in the seven months of winter about twelve tons of manure; and if foddered in summer about seven tons more. Thus a large ox would produce, altogether, about 19 tons in the yard. In feeding in boxes an ox of average weight, it was said, would produce about 11 cubic yards of manure in four months, or 33 cubic yards if kept constantly in a box for the whole year.

In reference to the value of manures from farm stock, it was remarked that horses was much superior to that from oxen, and that from oxen superior to that from cows, and that from old or full-grown animals far superior to that from young animals. A cow in feeding extracts a larger quantity of the nutritive qualities of food than an ox, because food passes more rapidly into the form of milk than that of muscle or flesh and fat. Again, nearly all the food consumed by full-grown animals goes to supply the natural waste of the system, whereas much of that consumed by younger ones is absorbed in the formation of additions to the bones, flesh and fat, and this is the reason why the richest manure is produced by animals already fat and full-grown.

In the feeding of horses it has been found, said Mr. Baker, that this animal produced in solid and liquid deposits taken together three-fourths in weight of what it ate and drank. A well-fed horse would give $9\frac{1}{2}$ tons of solid and liquid manure per annum; and if to this were added about $2\frac{1}{2}$ tons of straw or other litter, the whole amount made by a horse in a stable in the course of a year might be estimated at 12 tons.

In our former paper the two following results were obtained from collating a variety of observations made by different individuals: 1. That an average size cow, or one fed chiefly on hay and allowed water freely, will make about two and a half pounds of solid manure for each pound of hay, or its equivalent consumed, or, allowing one-fifth for difference between it and in the usual state of dryness, about two pounds for each pound of hay consumed. 2. That the value of the manure made by a medium sized cow in the course of a year would be according to the usual modes of estimating ammonia, potash and phosphoric acid, equal to between $20 and $23, or a little over $10 in the course of the six moths of winter.

A comparison of the somewhat loose estimates which we have quoted, with the results which we obtained as to *quantity* from collating several observations of the highest degree of accuracy and reliability, will furnish additional grounds of confidence in the conclusions at which we arrived. In making any estimates based on these conclusions as to the *quantity* of manure made by animals fed in stables or at distilleries during the winter, it should be recollected that our conclusions refer to medium sized animals, cows or cattle rather under than over the weight of 1,000 lbs. If the application is to be made to the case of large oxen, from 1,400 to 2,000 lbs., a corresponding allowance must be made according to the gross weight and the greater quantity of food consumed.

As it may seem to many that the estimate given in our former article, as to the *value* of the total deposits, solid and liquid, of a medium sized cow or ox during the course of a year, must be too high, we wish to remind such of the fact, that according to the usual modes of managing manure, far more than half its value is dissipated by exposure to rain, sun and wind, while the liquid portion is seldom saved at all. As manures are usually managed, there is little wonder that some should think them hardly worth hauling and spreading. The virtue has gone out of them.

Then, again, it should be remembered in estimating the value of manures that much, very much, depends on the nature of the food consumed. The more nitrogen there is in the food, the more ammonia will there be in the manure. A cow or ox fed on straw, poor hay, and no grain, will yield manure of much less value than one fed on richer food, with oil-cake, &c.—*Country Gentlemen.*

Keep the Stable Floors Clean.

We know divers people who take some pride in their horses and cattle, but are inveterate slovens in their stables. Their racks and mangers are so made that half the hay they give their stock is wasted under their feet. They don't clean their stables but once a week or fortnight.

We have, indeed, seen stables, where valuable animals were kept, not cleaned out during the winter, and the heels of the poor beast stood a foot higher than their fore feet in the latter part of the season. We once hired a barn—a nice, newly built barn—of a man for the winter, and when we went to put our stock into it, found that the horse stable sill was more than two feet above the ground, and the poor beast had to leap that to get into it, and fall down or make a leap every time they went out of it; and also, that full eighteen inches of solid horse dung had to be thrown out, taking a man half a day to do it before we could use it; besides repairing the entrance by a bridge that they could walk in and out upon. We scolded the owner soundly for laziness—it was nothing else—and he only answered that "he hadn't time to clean it, and did not see what harm it did the horses!" And yet when we came to settle with him in the spring, he wanted some dollars extra because we used a part of his barn door to mix cut feed upon, on the plea that in wetting it for mixing, it rotted the floor during the winter! His half a dozen loads of horse dung, seething and fermenting through a long hot summer, didn't rot the stable floor.

A stable where stock is kept should be cleaned out once a day, at least, and twice if the animals stand in it day and night. In all our stable practice, we clean the stable twice a day and shake up the bedding, let the weather be as it will. On the floors of our calf and sheep stables we scatter dry litter, and when thoroughly soiled and saturated, we clean it out and supply its place with fresh. The ammonia arising from the stale of stock in the stables, becomes, in a very short time, very offensive to them, as it is to ourselves. It penetrates their lungs and gives them disease. Its pungency affects their eyes, making them sore and irritable, and is a positive injury, to say nothing of the slovenliness of leaving the stables unclean. Cleanliness, indeed, is as necessary to beast as to man. No creature can thrive when fouled and besmeared with ordure.

Where horses (not mares) and oxen stand regularly, holes should be bored through the floor to let their stale run through on to muck below, or into a trench by which it may pass off and be saved. Otherwise, it remains under them to make them uncomfortable when they lie down, unless they have bedding enough to fully absorb it, which is not always convenient. Our own plan of stable flooring is to raise that part on which the animals stand two inches—the thickness of the plank—above the passage behind, and sloping from the foot of the manger back, to give a fall of one or two inches in the distance of six or seven feet of floor on which they stand, to admit the stale to pass off readily, as well as to let the droppings on to the lower level behind them.—*Maine Farmer.*

Absorbent Power of Soils.

Absorption, defined by Webster as "the act or process of imbibing by substances which drink in and retain liquids," is a quality possessed by all soils in a greater or less degree. And of this difference in capacity, especially as regards absorbing and retaining manures, something has long been known, and has given rise to the application of the terms "hungry" and "quick," to loose and gravelly soils, because they do not

long show the effect, and speedily manifest the action of manures, while clays were said to "hold" the fertilizing matters applied. The investigations of chemistry show that beside what would naturally result from the different mechanical action—the compactness or porosity of the soil—there are differences in their chemical affinities for acids, alkalies and gases, which vary their power of absorbing and retaining the elements of fertility derived from manures.

Loamy and aluminous soils were found by Prof. Way to possess the power, when used as a leach or filter, of retaining the ammonia, phosphoric acid, potash, etc., contained in the drainage of a London sewer—the very elements most valuable for manure—and to have the wonderful property, not only to select, but to retain these elements against every power naturally brought to bear upon them, save the growth of plants themselves. "A power," he remarks, "is here found to reside in soils, by virtue of which not only is rain unable to wash out of them those soluble ingredients forming a necessary condition of vegetation, but even these compounds, when introduced artificially by manures, are laid hold of any loss, either by rain or evaporation."

These conclusions seem to show that on most soils (one class of experiments was made with light loam) manure may be applied at any time in the season with equal good results—that there is no danger of loss when actually mixed with the soil, either by filtration or evaporation. Further experiments are needed to prove the absolute correctness of these conclusions to the general mind, but there are those who believe they may act upon them with safety. If established, much labor may be saved in the application of manures. They may be drawn in the fall and plowed under, or left spread upon the surface, or may be distributed in winter instead of immediately before planting and sowing, which is ever the most hurrying season of the year. For ourself, on clays or heavy lands, we would not hesitate to act upon these suggestions.

Some experiments tried in England several years since by Mr. Thomson, to ascertain the power of the soil to retain unimpaired in value, manure applied during winter, and also its power to hold in *suspension* the fixed ammonia of barnyard tanks and manure heaps, resulted in the following deductions;—1. That clay soils might be manured a considerable time before sowing without loss. 2. That light, shallow soils should not be manured heavily at one time; and the manure should be kept as near the surface as possible without leaving it uncovered. 3. That it is desirable to deepen the cultivated soil on all light land, as it thus gives it a greater power of retaining manure.

That all soils possess considerable power of absorbing and retaining manure, is well known; but the great question of the most economical application of different fertilizers is, and will long remain an open one, and one upon which every farmer can do more or less to satisfy himself by practical experiment.—Let those who can, throw light upon the subject, for it is one of large importance in agriculture.—*Country Gentlemen.*

Water Proof Clothing for Negroes.

We give from the *Scientific American* the following method of rendering negro clothing proof against dews and showers:

"Take one pound of wheat bran and one ounce of glue, and boil them in three gallons of water in a tin vessel for half an hour. Now lift the vessel from the fire, and set aside for ten minutes; during this period the bran will fall to the bottom, leaving a clear liquid above, which is to be poured off, and the bran thrown away; one pound of bar soap cut to small pieces is to be dissolved in it. The liquor may be put on the fire in the tin pan, and stirred until all the soap is dissolved. In another vessel one pound of alum is dissolved in half a gallon of water; this is added to the soap-bran liquid while it is boiling, and all well stirred; this forms the water-proofing liquid. It is used while cool. The textile fabric to be rendered water proof is immersed in it, and pressed between the bands until it is perfectly saturated. It is now wrung, to squeeze out as much of the free liquor as possible; then shaken or stretched, and hung up to dry in a warm room, or in a dry atmosphere out doors. When dry, the fabric or cloth, so treated, will repel rain and moisture, but allow the air or perspiration to pass through it.

"The alum, gluten, gelatine and soap unite together, and form an insoluble compound, which coats every fibre of the textile fabric, and when dry, repels water like the natural oil in the feathers of a duck. There are various substances which are soluble in water singly, but when combined form insoluble compounds, and *vice versa*. Alum, soap and gelatine are soluble in water singly, but form insoluble compounds when united chemically. Oil is insoluble in water singly, but combined with caustic, soda or potash, it forms a soluble soap. Such are some of the useful curiosities of chemistry."
Soil of the South.

Seventh Annual Meeting.

The United States Agricultural Society will hold its Seventh Annual Meeting in the Lecture Room of the Smithsonian Institution, at Washington city, on Wednesday, the 12th day of January, 1859, when the election of officers will be held, and the business required by the constitution of the Society will be transacted.

Officers and Members of the Society are respectfully notified to attend, and a cordial invitation is extended to State and other Agricultural Associations to send Delegates, that there may be a general representation of Agriculturists "in Congress assembled," to protect and sustain their interests, acting as a national organization on such matters pertaining to Agriculture as may be deemed appropriate. Gentlemen from other lands who may be interested in the acquisition and diffusion of Agricultural knowledge, are also invited to attend, and to participate in the proceedings.

The Medals and Diplomas awarded at the Sixth Annual Exhibition at Richmond, will be delivered to successful competitors, or their agents. The published volume of Transactions for 1858, will be delivered to Members of the Society, and to gentlemen connected with the Agricultural Press.

Important Agricultural topics will be publicly discussed, after introductory remarks by eminent scientific and practical agriculturists. Gentlemen having other topics pertinent to the advancement of Agriculture, which they may wish to introduce or to have discussed, will please refer them to the Executive Committee, through the Secretary, that a place may be assigned them on the daily programme.

Delegates are requested to bring copies of the publications of the Societies which they represent—one for the Library of the United States Society, and others for foreign and home interchange.

Propositions from cities at which the next Annual Exhibition of the Society is desired, will be received and considered.

The Business Office of the Society is in Todd's Marble Building, one door west of Brown's Hotel, Pennsylvania Avenue, where all interested in the cause of Agricultural improvement are invited to call when in Washington city. A large number of Agricultural newspapers, periodicals and reports, (liberally contributed,) are placed on file for public inspection, and the Library is also free to all who may desire to examine it. Models or Drawings of Agricultural Implements, and other objects of interest, are placed on exhibition without charge.

Gentlemen who may wish to become Life Members of the Society, can do so by paying or remitting ten dollars to the Treasurer, Hon. B. B. French, Washington city. This will entitle them without any further payments, to the full privilege of membership—among these are: free admission to all exhibitions of the Society, the annual volumes of published Transactions, the Monthly Bulletin, and the large and elegant Diploma. The fee for Annual Membership is two dollars, which ensures the receipt of the

Transactions and the Monthly Bulletin for one year.

The Southern Planter.

RICHMOND, VIRGINIA.

Happy New Year.

Since the issue of our last No., another year, with all its concomitant circumstances of joy, grief, and toil: of pleasures, disappointments, and trials, has fled into the dim shadow of the past. We may remember, but cannot recall its hours. Yet time has laid upon us the burden and responsibility of both the number and occupation of its days. Happy he who, in a retrospective glance, finds nothing to regret of greater moment than the increase of grey hairs, which serve to warn him of the sure approach of life's winter, and an honorable old age. Of time past, the recording angel has made up his account; and we trust that in his sympathy for erring humanity, he has "dropped a tear" over the list of our short comings, and "blotted out the record forever," leaving life's page unblemished by marks of misspent time.

In tendering to our patrons "the compliments of the season," we wish them the enjoyment of all the best blessings of a beneficent Providence, and that they may so occupy the hours of the year now before them, as to secure for themselves, and those dependent on them, an increase of happiness, prosperity, and contentment.

"That they may live thro' many a joyous year,
 While health and happiness their steps attend—
May sleep with lids unsullied by a tear,
 With naught to grieve the heart, naught to
 offend."

A few words as to our own connection with the large and respectable class of our readers, may not now be improper. For six months past, it has been our duty to lay before them whatever we could collect of an agricultural character, which, in our humble judgment, we deemed best calculated to benefit, instruct, or amuse them. Of the measure of success attending our efforts, we may not speak, but we may honestly say, we have done our best to acquit ourselves of the task with fidelity and diligence—while, with a painful consciousness of having fallen far short of our wishes in the scale of excellence, we may ask them to "pass our imperfections by."

To many of our subscribers we are indebted for words of encouragement and good will, which have been gratefully received as "words spoken in season." These cheer us on, and tend to make of our labors, a labor of love.

Thus may there ever be, between our patrons and ourselves, a reciprocity of kindly feelings, and good offices, while our time is profitably employed under the direction of the "Lord of the harvest." May we be gathered in His sheaves, and stored in His Garner, when time shall be no longer; and until this change shall come, may we never fail to attain the fullest fruition of a happy New Year.

Special Notice.
TO SUBSCRIBERS IN ARREAR.

To every subscriber who shall send us, *before the first day of February next*, the amount now due us, together with his subscription for *the present year*, we will send with the receipt Postage stamps sufficient to pay the postage on the volume for 1859.

We hope they will *all* avail themselves of this offer. There are *many* of them in arrear, and their prompt attention to this matter will greatly benefit us.

We have received a pamphlet copy of the Introductory Address of John F. G. Holston, A.M. M.D., Professor of Clinical Surgery in the National Medical College, on the opening of that Institution, delivered in the Hall of the Smithsonian Institute, October 18th, 1858, and published by the unanimous request of the students.

The speaker gives a succinct but lucid and graphic history of medicine, first as an art and then as a science, and enunciates the cardinal points upon which it rests. "The *last* point is, indeed," says the speaker, "the only one strictly scientific and of an endlessly progressive character," namely: "By the process of generalizing, to discover principles or primary truths applicable to the explanation of all observed phenomena." He repudiates, with merited scorn, the *isms* and *pathies*, the *nostrum monger-*

ing and *specialisms* of our day, as having their antitype in the superstitious empiricism of Egypt, and extols the science of medicine as a "Godlike science, studying the relation of cause and effect by a system of severe induction, and rallying all the sciences around her, as subservient handmaids."

Cosmopolitan Art Journal.

A quarterly, devoted to the diffusion of Literature and Art. Containing in the December issue a number of well written articles, among which we name the following:

Art in America; its History, Condition, and Prospects. By HENRY T. TUCKERMAN.

Character in Scenery; its Relation to the National Mind. By the EDITOR.

Santa Croce; The Westminster Abby of Florence. By O. W. WIGHT.

Nature's Lessons. By Prof. IRA W. ALLEN.

A Ballad; Dainty Jenny Englisheart. By T. B. ALDRICH.

The House with Two Fronts. By ALICE CARY. And *Body and Soul,* (Poetry.) By METTA VICTORIA VICTOR.

It is beautifully illustrated with a number of fine engravings, portraits, &c.; and as a whole, is a very creditable representative of the intelligence and taste of the association under whose auspices it is published. We commend it to every one who desires to cultivate a taste for the beautiful,—a natural instinct of every mind, which, by its educational development, expands its powers, liberalizes, ennobles, and purifies its sentiments, and becomes the source of unalloyed pleasure, as well as the handmaid of Virtue.

We tender our thanks to the Publisher, for a sheet containing lithographic portraits of the eight Bishops of the Methodist Episcopal Church, South. If they are all as true and life-like as the likeness of Bishop Early, whom we have the happiness to know, and to hold in the highest estimation, as well for his personal worth, as "for his work's sake," this publication must be greatly valued as a memorial of these self-denying men of God, who have dedicated themselves to His service in the ministry of the gospel, and to the promotion of the progress and extension of that branch of the Christian Church to which they belong.

We are much pleased with the first number of the "Virginia Farm Journal," and cordially extend to Mr. Crockett the right hand of fellowship. We hope he may be well recompensed for his efforts in the cause of Agriculture, and meet with abundant success in his undertaking.

To Subscribers.

In consequence of the change in the Proprietorship of the "Southern Planter," it is very important that our subscribers should remit the amount of their indebtedness with as little delay as possible.

The amount due from each subscriber is in itself comparatively trifling, but in the aggregate it makes up a very large sum, and if each subscriber will consider this as a direct appeal to *himself,* and promptly remit the amount of his bill, it will be of infinite service to us.

We commence sending with this number the bill to each subscriber who is in arrear, and shall continue to do so until all shall have been sent out. We ask, as a favor, a prompt response from all.

The bills are made up to 1st January next. The fractional part of a dollar can be remitted in postage stamps, or the change returned in the same. AUGUST & WILLIAMS.

To Postmasters and Others.

We are satisfied, that with proper exertion, any person who will interest himself for us, will be able to make up a list of *new* subscribers for the "Planter," in almost any neighborhood, in this or any other of the Southern States. We offer, as an inducement to those who are disposed to aid and encourage us in our efforts to extend the circulation of this paper, the following premiums in addition to our hitherto published terms:

To any person who will send us clubs of

3 *new* subscribers and $6,—

    The So. Planter for 1857.

6 *new* subscribers and $12,—

    The So. Planter for 1857 and '58.

9 *new* subscribers and $18,—

    The So. Planter for 1857, '58 and '59.

15 *new* subscribers and $30,—

    The So. Planter for 1857, '58, and '50, and a copy of the Southern Literary Messenger for one year.

To single new subscribers we will send *the present* volume, (commencing with the number for January, 1859,) at the low price of $1 50, *paid in advance.*

We call upon every one interested in promoting the progress and improvement of agriculture, to lend us his aid in contributions of original articles on practical or scientific agriculture, in order that our paper may continue to be worthy of the confidence and support of those who have hitherto so liberally sustained it, and to whose interests its pages will continue to be zealously devoted.   ·AUGUST & WILLIAMS.

THE HIDDEN WORLD; *Or the Induction of General Principles from a multitude of Diversified Forms or Appearances.* By ISAAC TAYLOR.

"THE THINGS THAT ARE UNSEEN ARE ETERNAL."

The main prerogative of the human mind is its power of gathering general principles from a multitude of diversified forms or appearances. This faculty, to a greater or less extent, developes itself in all men; but in some is so vigorous that it predominates, and gives law to the dispositions and pursuits; in such instances its exercise is attended with a pleasurable emotion of the most vivid sort. The pre-eminence of the faculty of generalization constitutes what is termed the philosophic character.

The delight wherewith minds of this class contemplate universal truths, or abstract laws, does not so much spring from perceiving that some general principal holds good and reappears in a great number of instances, that very nearly, or perfectly resemble, one the other; as from discovering the occult presence or efficacy of some such principle in a multiplicity of cases which have few points, or perhaps, no other point of alliance beside this one of their obedience to the same general law.

The more there is of external diversity, or unlikeness, or of apparent contrariety among the particular instances that are thus allied by their subjection to a common rule, so much the more of keen satisfaction or delight will be afforded to the mind when it detects the hidden principle of union. And not merely does diversity of *form* enhance the pleasure of generalization, but it is augmented, also, by mere remoteness of time or place. Thus, if we could glance for a moment at the surface of some world immensely distant from our own, and there recognize the operation of the same principles of life and organization with which here we are familiar, this perception of analogy would generate a pleasurable surprise, made the more intense by the recollection of the vast stretch, or wide empire of such common laws.

These elements of intellectual enjoyment are richly furnished by the studies of the naturalist. Now, it may be, he compares family with family of the vegetable and animal world; and, after marking the ostensible peculiarities of each, descends beneath the surface of their external differences, and lays open those great and uniform principles of mechanical or chemical structure, to which all are conformed; and (if the figure may be used) he listens, and hears all beings uttering, in their several dialects, one

and the same code of physical existence. Or, turning from the present system of things, the lover of nature explores the deep strata of the earth, gathers thence the fossil remains of long extinct tribes, and, with more pleasure than the vulgar can conceive of, or he express, brings to light the unvarying laws of animal organization, as they held their sway ages ago, among orders the most strangely unlike to the species of the recent world. Whether he looks to the extreme distances of space, or of time, the naturalist, after giving a moment to the obvious or common gratification that springs from novelty and diversity, seeks and soon finds the more lasting and substantial pleasures of reason, while marking the oneness and harmony of nature, even where her clothing and her colours, and her proportions have the least of uniformity.

If we might so speak, it is by her *diversities*, her gay adornments, her copious fund of forms, her sportive freaks of shape and colour, that Nature allures the eye of man, while she draws him on to the more arduous, but more noble pursuit of her hidden analogies. *Unlikeness* awakens his attention; *uniformity*, or simplicity, fixes and enchains it; and, by the pleasure it confers, ensures on his part the laborious investigation of abstruse principles.

While the human mind is thus employed, an insensible process goes on, the effect of which is gradually to invest general truths with a sort of majesty, as well as beauty; so that, at length, this new charm rivals and prevails over the graces and attractions of exterior diversity, and imparts more and more force and advantage to that which is occult, until it quite overpowers that which is visible.

Thus it is, that, in the course of philosophical pursuits, abstract principles come forth more into the light—stand out with more distinctness before the mind, and, ere long, the laws which at first were apprehended with some degree of painful effort, occupy it as pleasant and facile matters in the hour of relaxation, as well as engage it in the season of strenuous exertion. At last, whatever is universal prevails altogether over whatever is individual, and the rational faculty, getting released from the disturbance and fascination of things external—accidental —trivial, contemplates with open eye all that is great and permanent.

The whole evidence of our modern physical science serves to establish the belief (a belief in itself highly reasonable) that the mechanical and chemical laws which prevail in our planet, are common to other planets, and to other systems—even the most remote of them; so that, in *this* sense, the inhabitant of any one world would find himself at home in any other: just as the traveller, how much so ever he may be, for a moment, perplexed by diversity of climate, or strangeness of foreign manners, soon confesses that nature and man are essentially the same in the country he has reached, and the country he has left.

But, on the other hand, it cannot well be

doubted that the same principle of inexhaustible variety, which as we see, in our world, throws out so many thousand forms of beauty, has also its full play in other worlds, and takes its range as freely in one district of the universe as in another. If so, it follows that, could we visit and explore other regions, or were permitted to tread the fields of space, and to set foot, as pilgrims, upon distant spheres, each newly discovered world must amaze the eye, by its singular fashion, or peculiar aspect, or peculiar mould of beauty; each would present its proper and distinguishing *style* of symmetry and colour. Nevertheless, beneath all these diversities, and amid the confusion of these special graces, there would still be couched (as the supposition implies) the few great canons of organic combination; so that each planet of all the skies would at once challenge to itself an individuality, and confess its relationship, or bond of alliance, with all the rest.—

—And who shall duly conceive of that emotion of wonder and pleasure, with which the forms and contrivances of so many dissimilar worlds must present to a rational mind what may well be called the majesty or awful force and sanction of those few canons to which we find submission is made in all regions of the material system? In returning to our abode from an excursion such as we have imagined, the familiar objects that adorn it, ceasing to attract the eye by their individuality, would henceforward stand before us as the mere symbols of the abstract truths that had now gained possession of the mind.

We may safely employ the analogy which we have thus drawn from the material world, and transfer it, with its inferences, to the intellectual and spiritual system. And we institute our parallel as follows:—It is not to be questioned that the laws of the Divine Government (not less than the first principles of the material world) are one and the same in all places of the universe; for these laws are nothing else than *expressions* of the Eternal Excellence—its goodness, and wisdom, and purity. As in the Supreme Being there is no variableness, so neither can there be contrariety or opposition of purposes within the circle of his administration. Nevertheless, though the laws and ultimate issue of the moral system must be one and unchanging, and must challenge application to all possible cases, yet it is reasonable to believe that the modes under which this one purpose or rule of the divine government reaches its accomplishment are as various as the worlds wherein it is taking its course are many. In other words, we are compelled to suppose, on the one hand, that the intelligent universe presents an absolute *unity of principle;* and on the other, that it offers infinite dissimilarities of means and events. If each sphere or planet has its own physical character—its peculiar fashion and form, so, doubtless, has each family of intelligent beings its special destiny—its single and peculiar history, and its individual round of fortunes. The ways of Him who sits on the throne of universal dominion are "a great deep," and of his judgments or dispensations "there is no end."

Now, in the very same way that extensive generalization in matters of physical science imparts gradually to universal laws a predominance in the mind over visible appearances and single instances; so, by an analogy of principle, would an extensive knowledge of the intellectual and moral system, as it now exists, or has heretofore developed itself, in other worlds, produce a similar prevalence of abstract truths over the impression of particular facts. If a *moral* instead of a *physical* process of generalization could be pursued by the human mind in its passage from system to system; and if it could listen to the history, witness the condition, and learn the destiny, of thousands and thousands again of immortal tribes, whatever was uniform or fixed in the maxims of the divine government, and which presented itself ever and anew in every world, would, at length, assume to itself a paramount importance, and fill the faculty of rational contemplation almost to the exclusion of lesser objects.

Let it be granted that, for awhile—perhaps long—the spirit of the traveller through the universe would be overpowered by its emotions of amazement and curiosity, in contemplating so many diversities of social constitution—so much strange magnificence, so many new forms of greatness or splendour;—the energies—revolutions—adventures of innumerable families. This must be : but it is certain that a mind constituted like that of man, would, at length (if we may so speak) collapse, or fall in upon its centre; it must return, and take up its proper nature—its innate usages of generalization ;—it must court the calmness of *reason*, as a relief from the turmoil, and perplexity, and fatigue, of looking so much abroad. Then would commence that process of the understanding, which digests and simplifies multifarious objects, and by which the burden and distress of too much variety is relieved. Or perhaps, suddenly, in the full course of eager contemplation, the spirit would be arrested by the thought of *the universal law*, which (amid these changing scenes) was displaying its unchanging force; and, as with an instantaneous revulsion, it would at once pass over from things individual and visible, to things invisible and permanent.

In like manner, as from physical generalization, the beautiful (might we say, awful) simplicity of the material world fills the mind with a calm and elevated pleasure; so, and with much more power, would a similar process, carried on while the moral world at large was passing under the eye, bring in upon the heart those universal principles of the divine government which are the expression of the Divine Nature. These principles would gradually come forth from amid the innumerable instances of their efficacy; they would slowly and silently present themselves in a clearer and still clearer light; they would more and more be disengaged from anomalies or exceptions. The unchanging and unsullied glories of absolute purity, wisdom, and benevolence, would with an accelerating augmentation, prevail over the glare and show of individual objects. Whatever is limited, partial, temporary, contingent, accidental, must fade and become dim, or take its proper place of comparative insignificance. Meanwhile, though the SUPREME, who dwelleth in light inaccessible, were not visibly revealed, nevertheless his actual presence, as Ruler of all beings, would be declared in the brightness of his attributes; so that the issue of so large a knowledge of the moral and intellectual system must cause, to the rational spirit—a vanishing of the creation, with its diversities, and a manifestation of the Creator in his unchangeable perfections. Or otherwise to express the same thing, that which is " seen and temporal" would be lost in that which is " unseen and eternal."

Back Numbers of the Southern Planter Wanted.

See the advertisement of J. W. Randolph, on the first page of Advertising Sheet.

AGENTS.

Mr. FITZHUGH CATLETT is our authorized agent (at Guiney's Depot, Caroline County,) to receive money for us, and to give receipts. New subscribers are requested to leave their names with him, *daily, if not oftener*.

Mr. GEO. C. REID, is our agent in Norfolk, Va.

F. N. WATKINS, Esq., at the office of the Farmer's Bank of Virginia, at Farmville, is our authorized agent to receive money due for subscriptions to this paper, and to grant receipts therefor. Our subscribers in Prince Edward and the counties adjacent will please call on him.

Maj. PHILIP WILLIAMS is our authorized agent to receive subscriptions, and give receipts for us. See his card in our advertising sheet. Our subscribers in Washington City and Georgetown, D. C., will confer a favor on us by settling their bills with him.   AUGUST & WILLIAMS.

The Economy of Working and Gearing Teams.

Mr. Editor—In a former communication I merely hinted at the subject of "Centre Draught," or "The Proper Mode of Gearing Horses and Mules to the Different Vehicles and Implements to which they are worked."

The subject is one in which the community generally and the farming portion of it particularly is deeply interested. Indeed, all would be surprised to see, if I could succeed in demonstrating it, to what an extent they are interested in that which appears at first thought to be but a trifling, insignificant matter. We will assume, without pretending to entire accuracy, that the teams on each farm constitute one-tenth or one-eighth of the whole capital employed on it, requiring the humane and watchful care of their owner to keep them in that healthful vigor and state of flesh which will best develop their strength and activity, and enable them not only to perform well for the time being the work assigned them, but also to preserve them in a thrifty and improved condition that will ensure the long continuance of their ability to discharge their functions properly.

Their intrinsic value, as well as the duration of their service, all must admit, will greatly depend upon the care and protection accorded to them by their owner. Any means, therefore, by the adoption of which one-fourth of the power neutralized or wasted in the ignorant, careless, or injudicious use of these teams may be saved, not only adds proportionally to their value, but economises in like proportion the expense of maintaining them, as well as justifies the curtailment of the number employed. In regard to the gearing of horses or mules and oxen, I refer you to two articles which I published in the Southern Planter of January 1858. These articles explain how teams should be geared to ploughs, wagons, &c., but do not touch on the mode of attaching them to *carts*. On this subject, therefore, I now design to speak particularly. The draught line, as I have before stated, should pass from the shoulder of the horse to the junction of the back and belly band on the traces, precisely at right angles, in order that the pressure on the shoulder by the pulling of the horse may be so steady as to hold the collar and hames firmly in their proper place, thereby avoiding the fruitful source of the chafing and galling which disfigure, and often disable teams, by preventing the slipping of the collar up and down at each alternate step of the animal as he advances. Besides this, the right angle line from the shoulder to these bands, or the place where they should be (which is just behind the shoulder) is the one upon which the horse can exert the greatest amount of power and throw the greatest degree of weight; both of which are essentially necessary in pulling. This being a fact, demonstrated by practice, we will now say that long traces should be used to carts as well as to one-horse wagons, and should be attached to a swingletree in the same manner, in preference to hitching the hame on each side, with a few links of chain directly to the cart shaft. This mode requires the horse to pull the whole load first with one shoulder and then with the other, whereas pulling on the swingletree the pressure is kept up all the while on both shoulders, because the swingletree is fastened on a pivot in the centre, and varies to suit the walking motion of the horse. Again, the long traces can be so fastened by the back and belly bands as to get the power line of the horse, because they are flexible and the shafts are not, and hence the line of traction of the horse *cannot* be gotten when pulling by the shafts. The difference in the two modes is at least twenty-five per cent in favor of the traces. The mode of working one horse before another to a cart, *as practised*, is shocking. Against this practice, I adduce the following simple and plain reason, viz:

When a line is drawn straight from the centre of the resistance of the wheel and axletree to the pulling point at the girth where the traces crook *into the draught line* of the shaft horse, and another line is drawn from the same point of resistance of the wheel and axletree to the *pulling point of the girth* of the front horse where the traces crook upward into his draught line, —the two lines thus described, will be found very far from being parallel with each other. The line running to the front horse's girth will be found to be very much lower than the rear one, because more distant from the centre of resistance of the wheel and axle, and because the centre of resistance of said wheel and axle is not so high generally as the point at the girth where the crook takes place, unless the team be exceedingly low.

Now, instead of running the traces from the girth of the front horse straight on to the centre of resistance of the wheel and axletree, run them to the ends of the cart-shafts, where they generally fasten,— which is some six or eight inches higher than the proper or correct line, and the front horse will exert a part of his strength or power in pulling the load, and a part in pulling a burden on the back of the rear horse. The amount of the lost power of the front horse in burdening the rear one, and the rear one in being burdened by the front one, will be precisely in proportion to the amount of power exerted by the front horse, and the crook or angle (at the end of the shafts) of the line upon which said front horse is pulling.

The amount I will not undertake to determine here, for it is needless to the end I have in view. Suffice it to say, the loss is very great, and may be very easily ascertained at little or no cost. The remedy is too simple to need explanation. But if it be necessary, I will most cheerfully give it at some future day either by drawing or otherwise.

In conclusion, I would most seriously urge the users of horses to turn their attention to this subject. It is one fraught with momentous benefits, in accomplishing greater results with their horses, and in keeping them in better condition and causing them to be far more durable.

OBSERVER.

Compliment to Virginia Farmers.

In looking over a recent number of the Boston Congregationalist, we were very agreeably surprised to find in it the following complementary remarks on Virginia Farmers. We had seen in that paper so many things of a very different caste, whenever it has spoken of the South, that we were not prepared to find in its columns the testimony of a Northern man, who is impartial and independent enough to see and report things, just as he found them at the late Agricultural Fair in Richmond. We hope he will advise our New England brethren to visit the Southern Planters and take a *"South side"* view of things. It can do them no harm. Let us hear him:

"After enjoying a good and ample opportunity for observation, I feel no hesitation in saying, that physically, and socially, the Southern farmers are more genial and sociable than they are East or West, judging from observation. They impress a Northerner, that they enjoy life better, and are really and substantially, a happier people than the inhabitants of the East or West. I never saw so many large and well-proportioned men, physically, and such uniformity of genial, good-natured faces, as at Richmond. This quantity of graceful good-nature, was one of the most attractive, pleasing, and interesting characteristics of Southern farmers. Would that our excellent New Englanders, engaged in the same occupation, would cultivate the same genial graces. A sad face, certainly, ill becomes one who lives, and moves, and has his being among plants, and trees, and flowers, and fruits and grains, and singing birds, and shrilling insects, and creeping reptiles,—amid a world adorned with beauty, and vocal with song. If any class above all, have special reasons for being genial and cheerful, and sociable, and running over, as it were, with peaceful good-will toward all men, it is the farmers. For them, then, there is no really good apology for their going about with a sad countenance, and clad with silence, as it were, with a garment.

More skill is manifested in farming and gardening at the South, than I expected to see. In stock breeding, whether of cattle, or horses, or mules, New England would, most likely, come off second best in a fair comparison. In Short Horns and Devons, old Virginia and Maryland may challenge the East and the West, without fear of being beaten in quality. They rank high, also, in the production of fine horses, as was demonstrated at the Fair.

Sheep-culture and wool-growing have been recently and successfully introduced into some parts of Virginia. One farmer informed me that he had recently stocked his farm with about a thousand fine-wooled sheep, and now raises more wheat than when he kept no sheep. He finds them excellent renovators of the soil, in reclaiming worn land, and rendering it highly productive. He also said, that his wool brings three or four cents a pound in market more than Northern wool, because less " gummy."

Christian Observer.

Counsels to the Young.

Never be cast down by trifles. If a spider breaks his web twenty times, twenty times will he mend it again. Make up your minds to do a thing, and you will do it.—Fear not if trouble comes upon you; keep up your spirits though the day may be a dark one—

" Troubles never last forever,
The darkest day will pass away!"

If the sun is going down, look up to the stars; if the earth is dark, keep your eyes on heaven. With God's presence and God's promise, a man or child may be cheerful.

" Never despair when fog's in the air,
A sunshiny morning will come without warning!"

Mind what you run after! Never be content with a bubble that will burst; or a firewood that will end in smoke and darkness. But that which you cankeep, and which is worth keeping.

" Something startling that will stay
When gold and silver fly away!"

Fight hard against a hasty temper. Anger will come, but resist it strongly. A spark may set a house on fire. A fit of passion may give you cause to mourn all the days of your life. Never revenge an injury.

"He that revengeth knows no rest;
The meek possess a peaceful breast."

If you have an enemy, act kindly to him, and make him your friend. You may not win him over at once, but try again. Let one kindness be followed by another, till you have compassed your end. By little and by little great things are completed.

" Water falling day by day,
Wears the hardest rock away."

And so repeated kindness will soften a heart of stone.

Whatever you do, do it willingly. A boy that is whipped at school never learns his lessons well. A boy that is compelled to work, cares not how badly it is performed. He that pulls off his coat cheerfully, strips up his clothes in earnest, and sings while he works, is the man for me—

" A cheerful spirit gets on quick;
A grumbler in the mud will stick."

Evil thoughts are worse enemies than lions and tigers, for we can get out of the way of wild beasts—but bad thoughts win their way everywhere. Keep your heads and hearts full of good thoughts, that bad thoughts may not find room—

" Be on your guard, and strive and pray,
To drive all evil thoughts away."

The rough work of the world is sure to be done sufficiently well at the prompting of those motives which impel every man to do the best he can for himself. These universal motives take effect alike upon the lad who sweeps a crossing and upon an under secretary of state. Another class of the common interests of a community will be cared for and made good by those who, while laboring, in fact, for their fellow-men, are thinking only of their individual tastes in doing so. It is thus that much of the intellectual work of a people is prosecuted in the fields of philosophy, poetry, and the fine arts.

The Light at Home.

The light at home! how bright it beams
  When evening shades around us fall;
And from the lattice far it gleams
  To lure to rest, and comfort all,
When wearied with the toil of day;
  And strife for glory, gold, or fame,
How sweet to seek the quiet way,
  Where loving lips will lisp our name.

When, through the dark and stormy night,
  The wayward wanderer homeward hies,
How cheering is the twinkling light,
  Which through the forest gloom he spies!
It is the light of home, he feels
  That loving hearts will greet him there,
And softly through his bosom steals
  The joy and love that banish care.

The light at home! How still and sweet
  It peeps from yonder cottage door—
The weary labourer to greet
  When the rough toils of day are o'er!
Sad is the soul that does not know
  The blessings that its beams impart,
The cheerful hopes and joys that flow,
  And lighten up the heaviest heart.

From the Knickerbocker.

Rich Though Poor.

BY A. D. F. RANDOLPH.

No rood of land in all the earth,
  No ships upon the sea,
Nor treasures rare, nor gems, nor gold,
  Do any keep for me:
As yesterday I wrought for bread,
  So must I toil to-day;
Yet some are not so rich as I,
  Nor I so poor as they.

On yonder tree the sun-light falls,
  The robin 's on the bough,
Still I can hear a merrier note
  Than he is warbling now:
He's but an Arab of the sky,
  And never lingers long;
But *that* o'erruns the livelong year
  With music and with song.

Come, gather round me, little ones,
  And as I sit me down,
With shouts of laughter on me place
  A mimic regal crown:

Say, childless King, would I accept
  Your armies and domain,
Or e'en your crown, and never feel
  These tiny hands again?

There's more of honor in their touch
  And blessing unto me,
Than kingdom unto kingdom joined,
  Or navies on the sea:
So greater gifts to me are brought
  Than Sheba's Queen did bring
To him, who at Jerusalem
  Was *born* to be a King.

Look at my crown and then at yours
  Look in my heart and thine:
How do our jewels now compare—
  The earthly and divine?
Hold up your diamonds to the light,
  Emerald and amethyst;
They're nothing to those love-lit eyes,
  These lips so often kissed!

Oh! noblest Roman of them all,
  That mother good and wise,
Who pointed to her little ones,
  The jewels of her eyes.
Four sparkle in my own to-day,
  Two deck a sinless brow:
How grow my riches at the thought
  Of those in glory now!

And yet no rood of all the earth,
  No ships upon the sea,
No treasures rare, nor gold, nor gems
  Are safely kept for me:
Yet I am rich—myself a King?
  And here is my domain:
Which only God shall take away
  To give me back again!

Gentle Words.

A young rose in the summer time,
  Is beautiful to me,
And glorious the many stars,
  That glimmer on the sea;
But gentle words and loving hearts,
  And hands to clasp my own,
Are better than the brightest flowers,
  Or stars that ever shone;

The sun may warm the grass to life,
  The dew, the drooping flowers,
And eyes grow bright and watch the light
  Of autumn's opening hours;
But words that breathe of tenderness,
  And smiles we know are true,
And warmer than the summer time,
  And brighter than the dew.

It is not much the world can give,
  With all its *subtle art*,
And gold or gems are not the things
  To satisfy the heart;
But, O, if those who cluster round
  The altar and the hearth,
Have gentle words and loving smiles,
  How beautiful is earth!